"I mean, I was pretty smooth, you know."

I first moved to 116th Street when I was twelve-and-a-half. About two days after we moved in I came downstairs to sit on the stoop and that's when I met some of the other kids.

Fast Sam shook his head and looked at me like I was smelly or something. "Can you stuff?"

I knew what he meant. I could play basketball pretty well, but there was no way I could jump over the rim and stuff the ball. No way. I couldn't even come close.

"Yeah, turkey, can you?" They all looked at me.

"If I get a good start," I lied, asking myself why I was lying.

♪♪♪

OTHER BOOKS YOU MAY ENJOY

Fast Sam, Cool Clyde, and Stuff

WALTER DEAN MYERS

PUFFIN BOOKS

For Karen and Michael

PUFFIN BOOKS
Published by the Penguin Group
Penguin Young Readers Group, 345 Hudson Street, New York, New York 10014, U.S.A.
Penguin Group (Canada), 90 Eglinton Avenue East, Suite 700,
Toronto, Ontario, Canada M4P 2Y3 (a division of Pearson Penguin Canada Inc.)
Penguin Books Ltd, 80 Strand, London WC2R 0RL, England
Penguin Ireland, 25 St Stephen's Green, Dublin 2, Ireland (a division of Penguin Books Ltd)
Penguin Group (Australia), 250 Camberwell Road, Camberwell, Victoria 3124, Australia
(a division of Pearson Australia Group Pty Ltd)
Penguin Books India Pvt Ltd, 11 Community Centre,
Panchsheel Park, New Delhi - 110 017, India
Penguin Group (NZ), 67 Apollo Drive, Rosedale, North Shore 0745, Auckland, New Zealand
(a division of Pearson New Zealand Ltd.)
Penguin Books (South Africa) (Pty) Ltd, 24 Sturdee Avenue,
Rosebank, Johannesburg 2196, South Africa

Registered Offices: Penguin Books Ltd, 80 Strand, London WC2R 0RL, England

First published in the United States of America by Viking Penguin Inc., 1975
Published by Puffin Books, a division of Penguin Books USA Inc., 1988
This edition published by Puffin Books, a division of Penguin Young Readers Group, 2007

31 33 35 37 39 40 38 36 34 32

Copyright © Walter Dean Myers, 1975
All rights reserved

THE LIBRARY OF CONGRESS HAS CATALOGED THE VIKING EDITION AS FOLLOWS:
Myers, Walter Dean. Fast Sam, Cool Clyde, and Stuff.
Summary: New to 116th Street in New York, a young boy soon makes friends
and begins a year of unusual experiences.
[1. City and town life—Fiction. 2. New York (N.Y.)—Fiction.] I. Title.
[PZ7.M992Fas 1988] [Fic] 87-7355

Puffin Books ISBN 978-0-14-032613-0

Printed in the United States of America

contents

prologue

This is a story about some people I used to hang out with. It's funny calling them people. I mean they're people and everything, but a little while ago I would have called them kids. I heard that one of them, Gloria, got married about a month ago. I met her mother in the supermarket and she told me. I was really shocked. Gloria had moved away from the old neighborhood about a year and a half ago. Her father and mother had gotten back together, and they moved into one of those rent-controlled places where the State tells you how much rent you have to pay. Since her father got a decent job the guy really changed. I can dig him changing like that.

But, like I said, I was really shocked to find out that Gloria was married. I tried to imagine her married and I just couldn't. You know, you picture somebody in your mind and try to imagine them doing something different. It's hard. Like a guy who couldn't play any ball at all, all of a sudden becoming a professional ballplayer and signing up for a hundred thousand dollars or something. Not that Gloria wasn't okay or anything—it was just that when I thought of her I always thought of her just hanging out on the block and being fourteen. I said to myself, now how could she be married? Dig? Then I started thinking and I realized that Gloria was fourteen when I first knew her and that was a little over five years ago so she must be going on twenty now. And when I started thinking about Gloria I started thinking about the rest of the people—I'm going to call them kids—that I grew up with. I mean, they were a good bunch of people. Sometimes I think back on them and realize that I haven't come across a whole group of people like that since.

I don't want you to get the impression that my life is a drag or anything. I'm eighteen and I think I'm doing okay. But things change when you get older, I guess. It's harder to make friends because you end up asking more from everybody. You know, when you go out with a girl and you get serious you don't want her to go out with anybody else. Or when you get a job you want everyone else on the job to do their share. But when you're a kid you don't have to worry about things like that. At least I didn't have to.

I first moved to 116th Street when I was twelve and a half. I moved into this building about halfway down the block, which, I found out later, everybody called the safe house. (If someone from another block was chasing you and you made it to the safe house, they would never chase you inside. That was because they'd have too far to run to get *off* the block if your friends started after them.) Anyway, I moved into this house which was officially 81 West 116th Street. I moved into Apartment 4S. I really liked the apartment because I had a separate room. In fact, that's why we moved to 116th Street in the first place. I was twelve and my sister was ten and my mother said it was high time I had my own room. So finally my father found this place and we moved. My room was small but it was all mine. Sharon got our old dresser set and I got a new one. Things were really going well. It was just early fall when I moved in and I'd started school already, but I had to transfer to a new school called James Fenimore Cooper. It was an older school than the one I'd gone to, but that was okay because they had a really good music department and I played saxophone.

About two days after we moved in I came downstairs to sit on the stoop and that's when I met some of the other kids. I had a feeling they were going to be all right from the start because they started kidding around with me right away. They were a little older than me, about a year or so, but that was really together because I liked hanging out with older people. Most of them were thirteen at least and some even fourteen.

That day I went downstairs they were all wearing dungarees. They had patches on the knees, the kind you sew on, with funny little sayings or birth signs. One guy, a kind of dark-skinned dude with wide shoulders, had a Sagittarius patch on his right knee and a Leo patch on his left knee. One Spanishy-looking girl with long hair had butterflies all over her pants. It was a cool-looking group. All the guys wore sneakers and the girls had on sandals.

"Hey, man, what apartment you live in?" one guy with a real long head asked me.

"Four S," I said, trying to be cool.

"Can you play any ball?" Long-head asked.

"He can't play no ball," another guy said. "His feet go the wrong way. Look at him."

I looked down at my feet. They looked okay to me.

"Man, the cat that used to live in 4S sure could play some ball. You should be ashamed to even move into that apartment." Long-head shook his head and looked at me like I was smelly or something. "Can you stuff?"

"Do you mean dunk?" I asked. I knew what he meant. I could play basketball pretty well, but there was no way I could jump over the rim and stuff the ball. No way. I couldn't even come close.

"Yeah, turkey, can you?" They all looked at me.

"If I get a good start," I lied, asking myself why I was lying.

"I'll go get my basketball," a girl said. Later I found out her name was Gloria. A girl! I figured if the girls had basketballs around here, the guys must be fantastic. She ran into the hallway and into a first-floor apartment, and I started feeling terrible. My mouth got so dry I had to lick my lips. Just then another guy came up, and Long-head started right in again.

"Hey, Clyde, I want you to meet the new cat from Four S. I told him that the old cat that used to live there could play some ball, and he told us he could stuff."

"We ought to call him Stuffer," another guy said.

"Or how about Hot Stuff," Long-head put in.

I thought I felt pretty small then, but I really felt small when the girl came back dribbling the basketball. She passed it to me and I kind of smiled a little.

"Come on to the park, baby, so we can see you do your thing," she said.

"Don't call him baby," Long-head said. "His name's Hot Stuff."

I was really beginning to feel bad. The first day on the block and I had to go and say something stupid. But then this one guy, the one with the two birth signs on his dungarees, came and sat down on the same step I was sitting on. This put him just about in the middle of the group.

"Hey, look, we can deal with old Stuff later. Maybe

we'll take him to the park tomorrow and check him out. But we got to deal with Binky and that other cat."

"What do you mean?" Gloria asked, still holding the basketball. "What did Binky do?"

"Binky's supposed to fight this guy from the Milbank Center." Clyde—that was the kid's name—turned to me and spoke in a very calm voice. "We don't want Binky to lose the fight, but we don't want to get into a whole big fighting thing either, you know."

I didn't know about any of them, but I knew that *I* didn't want to get into any fighting thing. I also noticed that when Clyde talked he talked a little quieter than anybody else, and I wondered if he was older or something.

"What do you think, Sam?" Clyde was talking to Long-head.

"He got to fight the cat or everybody's going to think he punked out. Binky ain't no turkey, you know. Binky's a bad dude. Binky'll do one of these numbers, man. Bipp! Bipp! Bop-a rop-DOP! And the cat'll be knocked out, that's what's going to happen." Sam was hopping around and throwing punches at an imaginary person.

"Why do they have to fight in the first place?" I asked, trying to score off what Clyde was saying.

"Shut up, Hot Stuff!" Sam lifted a bony brown fist in my face, and I shut up but tried looking at him sideways. Looking at people sideways sometimes fakes them out.

"And don't be lookin' at me out the corner of your cross-eyed self either or I might have to knock you out. I knock out a man in a minute, you know!" Sam wasn't faked out.

"Yeah." Gloria put her hands on her hips and leaned forward. "You knock them out with your bad breath, you mean. Then you run. They don't call you Fast Sam for nothing, turkey!"

"Don't be playing with me, Gloria. I ain't kidding now." Sam tried to look tough and stuck his lip out a little. He looked so funny I wanted to laugh but I didn't, just in case he did knock people out. Well, you know, he was bigger than me.

"They got into an argument, some dumb thing about who said what about some girl, and then this cat from Milbank said he could beat Binky or anybody else on 116th Street, and this guy said he was coming over here to beat Binky's butt. They're getting into a thing over there at Milbank, you know. Gangs and all. I just don't want to get involved in it."

Just then Gloria's father came by with a bag of groceries, and he gave Gloria a soda out of it and asked if any of us wanted a soda. I wanted one but I didn't really know him so I said no, and Clyde said no and everybody said no except Sam. So Mr. Chisholm, who is Gloria's father, opened two sodas and gave one to Gloria and one to Sam and told Gloria to come in for dinner soon. Soon as he went in Gloria offered her soda around to some of the other guys and they each took a sip. And then Clyde asked Sam was he going to hoard his soda.

"Everybody done had some except Hot Stuff, here. And if he wanted some he should've asked Gloria's father while he was here." Sam gave me another dirty look.

"You don't be asking for all of people's stuff," Clyde responded. "Stuff's too cool for that. Right, Stuff?"

"Right," I said.

"He ain't too cool. You're cool, but he ain't cool. He's just dumb," Sam said, pushing his can of soda toward me. "And don't be spittin' all over the can, either."

"He do look a little weak in the head," Gloria added.

Well, that's how I got to meet the first people on the block. And those three, Fast Sam, Cool Clyde, and Gloria, turned out to be just about my best friends. Oh, they put me through a lot of things. The next day they made me go to the basketball court and try to stuff. I couldn't even come close and they all laughed. Especially Sam. He had to roll on the ground and kick his feet in the air and really carry on. Gloria and Clyde got me on pretty good, too. Afterwards we shot a round, and I could see that Sam was really a good basketball player. Everything he did seemed to be effortless. Clyde wasn't bad, but I was a little better than Gloria. A little. Anyway, that's how I got to meet them all, and that's how I got to be called Stuff instead of Francis. I dug that. Me. Stuff.

miracles of modern science

1 *I remember there was a long time when I thought modern science wasn't nothing but some jive stuff,* and that was because the only thing it ever did for 116th Street was to get everybody in jail. And on 116th Street we could get in jail being downright primitive—we sure didn't need new ways. I wasn't the only one in jail so don't think I'm just getting my thing off my chest either. Butch was in jail, Angel was in jail, Fast Sam, Binky, Light Billy, Dark Billy, and Clyde. Now the key to the whole mess was Binky and Clyde. Clyde because he was more or less the coolest guy on the whole block and you just know that if he's in jail something's got to be wrong. And Binky because it was his ear that got us in jail in the first place. His ear and that jive modern science stuff. Then again, it could have all been Clyde's fault because he was the guy that brought science into it in the first place. But like everything else Clyde did, it was cool at the time. Let me run it down right quick.

Clyde had told us that Binky and this guy from Milbank Center both liked the same girl. Now what they saw in her I don't know because she really wasn't that pretty or anything. As a matter of fact, you know what she looked like? That cat on the Quaker Oats box. Honestly! You imagine that cat having an Afro and you got Debbie. Anyway, they were both digging Debbie. You just know that sooner or later they were going to get into it. And both of these guys were bad. Binky could beat just about anybody on 116th Street. In fact, he *had* beat everybody on 116th Street except Clyde and Fast Sam. Clyde didn't fight. Ever. And if you got that guy into a corner he could make you feel so bad that you felt like a punk for hitting him. And Fast Sam was another story. He was so good at athletics that nobody wanted to try him. But if he had any doubt about it at all he'd run. And nobody on any block in the world was going to catch him. Especially when he was scared. And dig this, he almost always wore his sneakers to give himself an extra edge.

So anyway, Binky was bad. But this other guy was bad, too. His name was Robin and he had a scar across his forehead about two inches long. When he got mad that scar would start twitching. Clyde said he got that scar when him and his boys were walking through

Mount Morris Park and the Valiants caught them. He only had three of his boys with him and some girls, and there were about seven Valiants. He told his boys to take off and get some help while he slowed down the Valiants. So his boys took off and he fought the seven Valiants all by himself until his boys got some help. When they got back, Robin was still fighting the Valiants. His forehead was cut from being hit in the head with a bottle, but he was still on his feet. Now you know the guy is plenty tough. So what do we have? Two tough guys, Binky and Robin. Both liking the same girl, Debbie.

So one day we're all sitting on the stoop arguing about who was the best basketball player, Doctor "J" or Bob McAdoo, when Binky, Cap, and Royal come around the corner. Everybody said hello and Binky was rapping about how he thought McAdoo was better than the Doctor and all and just fell into the conversation.

Then from the other corner comes Robin and some of his boys. He only had a couple of his boys with him so we knew that there wasn't going to be any heavy stuff. So Robin comes bopping up and he stops about five feet away and hooks his thumbs in his belt.

"Hey, man," Robin says, looking dead at Binky, "I want to talk with you."

Gloria, who had been sitting on the stoop reading a comic book, got up and called some other girls over and said there was going to be a fight. You know how some girls are always ready to see somebody get their head whipped. She ran up to the top of the stoop and started calling all the other girls over and yelling that there was going to be a fight. So everybody came over and stood around.

"What you want to talk to me about?" Binky says. My man got his head laying over to one side like Paul Newman in *Butch Cassidy and the Sundance Kid*, and his hands were folded in front of him.

"I heard you was talking about me, man. And I don't dig people talking about me behind my back." That's what Robin said even though everybody knew they was going to fight over Debbie. But I don't think they wanted to admit fighting over a girl.

"Your name's Robin, right?" Gloria asked. Gloria was one of those girls that was always signifying—saying something to get something started or to make somebody mad.

"That's right," Robin said, rolling his eyes in Gloria's direction.

"You know, Binky, I think you were wrong," Gloria went on. "Robin looks like a nice cat. I don't believe half those things you said about his mama."

"Say what? What you say about my mama, man?" Robin's scar was twitching and the veins started standing out on his neck.

"I didn't say anything about your mama, Robin. She's just signifying, that's all."

Now everybody knew that Gloria was just signifying, but we didn't figure Binky to back out. If he got beaten it was one thing, but if he backed out he'd be letting down the whole block. I mean, if you're the baddest dude on the block you've got responsibilities. If you got the weight you got to take the freight. Even Robin was surprised because he had heard that Binky was a bad dude, and he called Binky a punk.

Robin could say "punk" so *mean*. He'd hesitate just a little bit before he said it, see, then his lips (and he had some big lips, too) would kinda curl up at the side and he'd shake his head and just let the word drip off his bottom lip. *"Punk!"*

"No, really, man. I didn't say anything about your mother. Please, you have to believe that."

"Well, just see that you don't either," Robin said. "And don't let me catch you on 118th Street no more either."

Well, we felt pretty bad about the whole thing, see. I'd heard Clyde and Sam and them say Binky was really tough, but I figured now that maybe Robin was just a lot tougher. Everybody was looking at Binky like he was supposed to do something but no one said anything. Even the girls, who were signifying in the beginning, didn't say anything when it seemed Binky was backing out of a fight. But just then Binky made his comeback.

"Look, Robin, I don't want to argue with you. I believe in equal opportunity for people who've been in terrible accidents, and from the way you look, I can see your face has been in just about the most terrible accident I've ever seen."

Everybody jumped up behind that. Binky was going to stand up to Robin after all.

"What did you say, man?" Robin's boys backed off because they knew the fight was on.

"I said if you were any uglier they'd put your face in a museum and sell tickets to gorillas." Binky stood up. "The worse thing I could say about your mama is that you're her son. And hasn't anybody told you yet that that toe-jam you keep between your teeth don't do nothin' for your breath? If you ask me you must be the retarded son of the Heartbreak of Psoriasis."

Right then and there it was on. Robin threw a punch at Binky and the fight started. They fought from Lenox Avenue, down one side of the street, all the way to Seventh Avenue, and then fought back on the other side. These cats weren't playing, either. Robin was throwing punches and beating Binky upside his head something terrible. But Binky had heart and hung in there. I mean, Robin was hitting him so hard that *I* wanted to cry. Binky's nose was puffed up and his lip was cut. He looked terrible. But he was taking Robin's stuff.

Then it started to turn around and Binky started to get his stuff together. Binky didn't even know how bad he really was until he got into the fight with Robin. Man, he got his stuff together and commenced to kick rump. He went to work on Robin like he was a bricklayer or something. No emotion. Nothing. Just went to work, doing his job. Wherever Robin looked there was a fist coming at him. He must have thought there were two or three guys fighting him. You could see when it turned around, too. At first, when Robin had his stuff together, he was saying things like "How's that, baby?" and "What do I look like now, punk?" But Binky had shut him up good and he wasn't saying anything now. After a while you could see the fear creep into his eyes. He looked pitiful, really. And all the girls were standing on the side signifying. Especially Gloria.

"Hey, Binky, you forgot this is national Be Nice to the Ugly Week!"

And everybody would crack up and even Robin's boys smiled a little. But that's when the real mess started. Because Binky knocked Robin down. Bam! Robin got up real fast and Binky knocked him down again. Bam! This time Robin just lay on the ground, figuring the fight was over. But Binky kicked him on the leg and he had to get up. This time he was crying. He knew he didn't have no win so when he got up he just charged at Binky and they both went down to the ground. They rolled around a little bit, and all of a sudden Binky started hollering. We couldn't figure what was happening because Robin wasn't throwing any punches and Binky was just hollering to beat the band. Finally he got Robin off of him, punched him in the mouth, and then grabbed the side of his head. Robin took off, running down the street, glad to be out of the fight.

Everybody gathered around Binky to see what was wrong, and that's when we found out that Robin had bit part of his ear off. No lie. Part of his ear was off. You couldn't see it too clear because of all the blood and everything, but you could tell it was off.

Everybody was ooing and ahing and saying dumb things and being like 116th Street in general. That's when Clyde had to stick his two cents in.

"Hey, man, dig. I read in *The New York Times* about this dude that got his finger cut off and they rushed his finger to the hospital and they sewed it right back on."

"You a cold dude, Clyde," said Light Billy. "The cat got his ear bit off and you talking about . . . oh."

It finally hit Light Billy what Clyde was talking about. It hit everybody else the same time. Then Clyde sort of took things over.

"Don't nobody move," he said, "so we won't step on Binky's ear. Just look around real careful."

"Suppose Robin swallowed it?" Gloria asked.

Well, that was kind of funny but nobody wanted to crack up. Binky was like a hero and you didn't want to crack up on some cat that was a hero just because he got his ear eat up.

At any rate one of the girls found his piece of ear under a car. I don't know how it got under the car unless Robin had just spit it out when he started to run. So they wrapped that piece of ear in a Kleenex and gave it to Fast Sam and he took off to the hospital. I mean he was moving. Binky and everybody else was running toward the hospital, too. I mean *everybody* else. That might have been our mistake, I don't know. We hit the hospital and ran into the emergency room and everybody started talking about how Binky got his ear bit off by Robin, and Clyde was shouting something about how he read all about it in *The New York Times*, when the first thing we knew they shut the emergency room doors from the inside and locked them and the place was full of police. They started cracking heads and dragging us out of there. The next thing you know, there we are, in jail. Charged with disturbing the peace, rioting, and everything else they could think about. They made us roll up our sleeves and stuff to check out whether we were junkies or anything.

They had this little Chinese doctor down there and he said he was treating a patient when a bunch of us hoodlums came in and tried to take the place over. So we finally got everybody quiet and told the sergeant about Binky's ear. And Binky said he was going to handle his own case and then appointed Clyde to be his lawyer. Clyde said they wanted to press charges against Robin for being a cannibal but first they wanted to have exhibit one sewn back on Binky. Exhibit one, of course, being the rest of his ear.

The sergeant asked where the ear was now, and Fast Sam fished it out of his pocket. It had come out of the Kleenex and had got some dirt on it from Fast Sam's pocket, and Binky wanted to punch Fast Sam in the mouth for not having any respect for his ear, and Fast Sam told him he'd better shut up before he bit his other ear off. Well, the doctor looked at the ear and wiped it off and then he said it was too late, that they couldn't sew it back on. He said something else, too, about how you could only stick on certain parts of the body and that part of the ear wasn't one of the parts. But by that time I wasn't even interested. I mean, here he's giving us this scientific talk and everything, and the only thing that science had ever done for any of us was to get us in jail.

Finally, after everything was explained and the sergeant was satisfied, they let us all go. Then we all went back to 116th Street. Modern science had got us in jail for a little while but it broke up the day. That's something, right?

That was really the first thing I did with the guys from 116th Street. And afterwards, when we sat around and talked about it, I really felt that being in jail was the best part in a funny way. Because if I hadn't run down and gotten myself in jail then, we wouldn't have done anything together. And it seemed to me that it was what you did that made you part of the group. More than if you had a lot of friends.

We didn't have to stay in jail for very long, either. Just about long enough to say we'd been there. And after that I found out that they all just accepted me even though I was new and all. But even so, it took a long time to really know them well. I hadn't, until then, really known anyone well except Sharon, my sister. And, as I said before, I knew her too well because we used to sleep in the same room. Everybody else I played with or went to school with and everything, I knew *about* but really didn't *know*. I never knew what anyone was thinking or how they felt. Sometimes you knew if somebody was hurt or something like that because you could see them crying. Or if they laughed you could see that, but all the in-between things, like not hurting but feeling sad, or not laughing and feeling happy, you couldn't tell. And since most people most of the time weren't crying or laughing, you couldn't tell about them most of the time.

Now for some people that's really not too important, I guess. At least I never heard anybody else running around talking about knowing how people felt. But to me it was pretty important. You know why? I really wanted to know if they felt like me. Sometimes I thought that some of the kids I knew, or kinda knew, didn't feel the same way about things that I did. I don't mean they didn't like the Mets or anything like that, but they didn't feel sad about things that made me feel terrible. And things that made me happy sometimes didn't make other kids happy.

Okay. Now the real problem (and it always takes me a while to get to the real problem) is that I'm kind of scary. If something happens that's a little scary, then you know I'm one of the people that's going to get scared. And I cry easy, too. At any old dumb thing. Sad movies or sad television shows, for instance. That kind of thing. Sometimes if I see a little kid getting beat up by a big kid, then I start crying for the little kid. Once I walked right up to a big guy who was picking on this little kid and told him he shouldn't. He bloodied my nose. Now I just feel bad and walk away.

But on 116th Street I got to know a lot about how people felt. We all did, I guess. And it was real cool. I didn't *always* know how they felt but I did sometimes. Also, I got to talk about it some. Or listen about it, really, because that's what I usually did. Listen. I was about the best listener around.

the funeral

2 *The next thing that happened on the block was very sad.* I didn't ever have anything sad happen to me personally. And when I saw it happening to other people I didn't understand it very much. Sometimes I think you have to live through something yourself before you can really understand it.

Cap was the first one to spread the news that Mr. Jones, Clyde's father, had been killed. His mother had gone down to the hospital with Clyde's mother, and when she called Cap to tell his father that she'd be getting home late she told him that Clyde's father had died in the hospital.

"How come he died?" Gloria asked.

"I don't know exactly, but there was some kind of an accident. My mother said something about a fork-lift truck falling over. Anyway, they took him to the hospital and then he died." Cap shrugged his shoulders.

"Where's Clyde?" somebody asked.

"He's over to his aunt's house," Cap said. "I didn't want to see him, you know. He was crying and everything."

Clyde's father was buried at the New Hope Memorial Cemetery in Long Island. Clyde was almost fifteen and had never been to a funeral before. The next day, when he came out on the stoop, he said that he couldn't remember all the things that had happened. All the time he was talking it looked as if he might cry any minute.

"They take so long. You have to sit around and wait for everything. First we had to wait for the funeral cars and for everybody to show up and everything. My mom was crying and my aunt was crying." Clyde was looking down at the ground and twisting his foot like he was trying to grind out a cigarette. "I had seen my mother cry before, you know, when she got real mad she'd cry, or that time when she cut her finger she cried, but she cried different this time. She cried so soft. You could hardly hear her. She was crying so private that it hurt, you know?

"Anyway, then you got to ride to the church and everybody looks at you and then Bishop Glover says that people should ask God to help you. Then the choir sang 'Just a Closer Walk with Thee.' That was my father's favorite hymn. Then you get up and walk past the coffin—they had the lid up . . ."

Clyde was crying and Gloria gave him her handkerchief.

"Then I looked at him laying there, and there wasn't anything I could do. My mother was crying and Kitty was holding my hand, and she was crying, and she was scared, too. Then after that we went out to the cemetery—that doesn't last too long. Then we came back. And it was a nice day. Came down Fifth Avenue and some guys were playing stickball in the street. I still can't think of him as being dead. I keep thinking of him sitting in the living room and drinking iced tea. He always drank iced tea when he watched the ball game. Just saying that somebody is dead doesn't make it any more real. The only thing that makes it real is Mama sitting up at night and reading from the Bible and crying to herself. That makes it real. You know?"

We all nodded and I saw that everybody else was as sad as I was.

Clyde told me much later that the first day back at school he was surprised to find out that most of the people in the school, teachers and children, didn't know about his father. A few that did said something but most didn't. And even around the block no one spoke about it, and after a while things were pretty much like they always had been. Except that his mother, who hadn't worked before when his father was alive, began to look for a job. Sometimes she wouldn't get home until after six o'clock. Kitty, his sister, was staying with his aunt until her mother found a job and made other arrangements. So when Clyde saw Fast Sam and me one day and it was raining too hard for us to sit on the stoop and talk, he asked us to come upstairs with him, not wanting to be alone until his mother came home.

"Hey, man, that's a good idea. We can go up to your house and drink sodas while we rap," Fast Sam said, thinking about food as usual.

We put on a soul station and Clyde looked into the refrigerator to see if they had any sodas. They had one full can and one half can he'd started yesterday. Clyde gave Fast Sam the full soda and took the other for himself. I didn't want any.

"So what's been happening, man?" Fast Sam's throat bobbed up and down as he tilted his head back and guzzled the soda.

"Nothing much. My mother's looking for a job."

"Yeah, look, I haven't said anything to you about your father, but I'm really sorry he died, you know."

"Thanks."

We sat for a long while without saying anything. We didn't know what to say. Fast Sam, who was a good dancer as well as the fastest guy in the neighborhood, snapped his fingers in time with the music.

"Say, dig, you know the center's giving a dance next week. Why don't you come?" Fast Sam asked.

"I don't know." Clyde looked down at his sneakers. "I'm not really in a mood to dance."

"It's easy for me to say, but why don't you try to get yourself in a mood? You can't keep yourself down forever. You're about the coolest dude I know, man."

"I don't feel cool. I feel like I've got a heavy weight in the middle of my stomach. No jive. That's just the way I feel. When I walk around a few hours, go to school and whatnot, I get so tired I can't even stand up. I feel like I should have done something. I mean, my father's dead and I—" Clyde's eyes began to get teary and he couldn't talk for a while. "Hey, I'm sorry," he said finally.

"Nothing wrong about crying because your father died, man. I can understand that. What do you mean, you think you should do something?"

"I don't know. My father died and he's gone and I can't say anything to him. When I got to the hospital he was already gone—that's the word my mother used—and I couldn't say anything."

"What did you want to say?"

"Nothing then. But now I wish I could say something like . . . you know, that I dug him and appreciated him and that kind of thing. I wish I could do something now, I guess."

"Well, if you make something of yourself, and all that kind of thing, you'll be doing something. That's what you got to do. Ain't really nothing else you can do except living like he was still alive and being cool to your mama. All that good doing stuff. What are you planning to take in college?"

"I don't know," Clyde said, finishing his soda. "How about you?"

"Man, I ain't going to college."

"Why not?"

"Well, I'm not taking a college course. I'm taking a commercial course. Everybody ain't got your smarts, man. Like you knew about getting that cat's ear back on and things—even if it didn't work out too cool at least you knew about it. My old man says that he'd like me to go to school and he'd try to get the bread together, but I don't really think he can."

"I'm not taking a college course, either. I just never gave it a lot of thought. You know, college seemed to be for cats that wore them button-up sweaters. Never really was that down. I don't know."

"Hey, baby." Fast Sam put down his soda, sliding it away from where I could reach it. "You're my main man, ain't you?"

"Yeah?" Clyde looked up and his eyes were red.

"We been tight since we been about this high, right?" He held his hand, palm down, about a foot above the floor.

"Yeah, Sam, I guess so."

"Then you can't be letting yourself down, man, because you'll be letting me down, too. Dig? I don't have your smarts. You know that and I know that, or maybe I do and just can't use them the way you do. But I'm proud of you. I can check you out and say, 'Hey, dig that little black dude doing his thing.'

You know, a lot of cats around here kind of lay their problems on you. Some cat uptight about this, some cat uptight about that. You know, if heavy cats like you be giving up, what am I suppose to do?"

"Hey, Sam, you can make a guy feel good when you want to." Clyde looked at Sam and gave him a little rap on his arm. They were so close to each other that I really wished I wasn't there. "Look, you think I can make a college program?"

"Yeah, I think so. And even if you can't, I think you can scare the daylights out of it if you don't get it."

"I guess I'll have to give it that big try. My mother would dig it, my father would have liked it, too."

"You'll dig it, too," I added. I was surprised to hear my own voice.

"Hey, little brother. Hey, Stuff. Maybe I will."

Clyde reached over and got Sam's hand and mine, and we all clasped our right hands together. I got so worked up I started crying and everything, and I would have died, I mean really died, except that I saw Clyde and Sam were crying, too. And then I got a funny feeling that being a man wasn't everything I thought it was. Because I wasn't ashamed of crying with these guys.

"Crying is feeling, baby, ain't nothing wrong with that." Sam had seen me trying to hold back the tears. "Ain't nothing wrong with that at all. Are you hip?"

"I'm hip," I sniffled, and we all slapped hands.

the dance

3 *People are funny. Here I am digging Sam from today, back on into yesterday and on into tomorrow.* Why? Because he was such a heavy dude in a light way. He came on so heavy when he was talking to Clyde about going on to college and everything. And he came on in a way you could understand. And then the next thing he did was to come rapping on my door with a big idea about how he and I should get Clyde to go to this dance and enter the contest with Gloria. He said that if Clyde won the contest he'd really feel good, and even if he lost it would take his mind off his father. I wasn't too sure about that. If a guy's father dies you don't go running up to him and talk about how he'd like to go dancing. We called Cap and asked him what he thought and he came

over to the house. It didn't take him long because
he just lived next door.

"You got to be kidding, man. I mean really! The
cat just lost his father a couple of weeks ago. He ain't
supposed to be out dancing. You guys got no heart,
no smart, and the part you playing is wrong." Cap
stood up and started scratching his nose the way he
always did when he was excited. "You must thrive on
jive. Man's heart's broken and he wrapped up in
misery and you talking about going to a dance. The
man's trying to get himself together in his hour of
need, and you trying to make him bleed. He ain't got
no chance in the world of winning the fifty dollars
so he's going to throw away his two dollars and fifty
cents plus the two dollars and fifty cents for his
woman. Let alone showing disrespect for his poor
departed father. The only father the cat ever had in
his whole life." He was really working on his nose now.
"I mean, can't you dudes think at all? I know what's
wrong. You see, it ain't your father that's passed on
to his reward so you don't care. Come on, man, admit
it! You don't care! Do you? Do you?"

"Hey, we care," Sam said. "Maybe we just made
a mistake."

"A mis-stake. You got to be jiving. Look, are you
going out to some dance when your father die?" Cap
got right up in Sam's face and gave him a look that
would turn chocolate milk into sour cream. "Well,
would you?"

"You don't have to get personal, dude." Sam gave Cap a look right back. "I don't want to have to knock you out."

"Yeah, yeah. Later." Cap just walked out of my room backwards and very slowly, looking at me and Sam like we really weren't very much. Then he closed the door and split.

I didn't say very much and Sam didn't say very much. In fact, we didn't say anything. Then, finally, Sam said something.

"Damn!" he said.

"Yeah." I almost said damn, too.

"Let's just forget the whole thing, man," Sam said. "I sure wouldn't be out dancing if my pops kicked."

"Yeah. It sounds terrible to even think about winning fifty dollars. You know. Fifty pieces of silver."

"Twenty-five. I got the application already." He reached into his shirt pocket and unfolded the application which announced the dance and the contest. The prize was either twenty-five dollars in cash or a portable tape recorder that played eight track tapes.

"Well, why don't you enter the contest?" I asked. "You can take Gloria and maybe you and her can win."

Sam's face broke into a big grin. I could see why his head had to be so long. If I had a grin that big it would meet in the back of my head. "And we got two days to practice, too. We could do one of these numbers."

He got up, turned up the radio, and started dancing. First he spun to the left, then he spun to the right, did a little bit of the Cosmic Slop, threw out a few moves from the Soul Robot, and then fell to the floor in a bad split and came up so fast and smooth I almost forgot he went down. No doubt about it, Sam was the best dancer on the block and probably in the neighborhood.

"Ain't that together, baby! Come on, tell me how good it was because you know you want to. I know it was good." Sam put out his hand and I gave him five.

"Now if you can get Gloria to go with you, you got it made," I said.

"If? What you mean *if?* She be a fool not to want to go to a dance with Fast Sam. Because the way I spin she got to win." Sam spun around and did a little dip. "The way I move she got to groove."

He wiggled his hips and shoulders and snapped his fingers and I could almost hear the music.

"*If* ain't even in my dictionary. I better break the good news to her gently because I wouldn't want to give her no heart attack. She's liable to pass out as it is. I wish I was one of them schizophrenics and had me a split personality. Then I'd say 'later' for Gloria and go to the dance with myself. Now wouldn't that be bad? Whew! Outa sight. Gloria, baby, here comes Fast Sam to spread the word of joy to you. And, Stuff, you be ready to catch her if she pass out."

We met Gloria on the stoop and Sam broke the glad tidings to her.

"You pimply-faced, big-nosed, wide-mouthed, bug-eyed, bad-smelling, pigeon-chested fool! If I got hit by a car you couldn't take *me* to a hospital."

"Wha?" Sam's mouth fell open. "Who you going with? Whoever they are they can't dance like the Sam. You know that."

"Will you get out of my face with your stupid self?" Gloria just about spit out the words. "I'm not going to that stupid dance at all. Especially with no . . ." Suddenly she started crying and pushed past Sam and went into the house. Sam looked at me and I looked at Sam.

"What got into her, man?" Sam asked, looking at the empty doorway where Gloria had disappeared.

I just shrugged. Gloria had a way of putting people down but she never seemed to mean it. She used to signify a lot. And she was so good at it that you didn't mind being put down, really. And she never picked on one person *all* the time. Not only that, Gloria would always ask about your parents or how you were doing in a way that really made you feel like she meant it. I looked over at Sam and he just stood there. I told him to close his mouth before all the flies in the neighborhood dropped in.

"Look at me, man." Sam stuck his face right up close to mine. "Is my nose on wrong, or something? Maybe my eyes are lop-sided. How I look?"

"You look the same to me," I said.

"Well you hear me say anything that I didn't hear me say?"

"No."

"Well what's the matter with that girl, then? What she so huffed up about?"

I thought that perhaps something had happened between Gloria and Sam that I didn't know about. Maybe they'd had an argument or something. If they had, I decided, it wasn't any of my business.

"Hey, Sam, you and Gloria have an argument or something?" I asked anyway.

"No, so I don't see why she had to jump so nasty." Sam walked over toward the doorway and I thought he was going to follow Gloria, but he just sat on the stoop and began to pound his fist into his hand. "I oughta go tell her off."

"Why?" I asked, not really knowing if I should be pushing my luck. "Are you mad?"

"'Cause I dig Gloria. Me and her's been tight for a long time, you know. I mean, we don't go around kissing or anything. I don't believe in a lot of kissing and stuff like that, but we been to the movies twice this year already. We saw the Kung Fu movies with that Chinese cat that died, and then we saw *Shaft Goes to Disneyland* or something like that. I even paid her way for the Kung Fu movie."

"She know you like her?" I asked.

"What I look like, a fool?" Sam gave me his sideways look. "You go around and tell some chick you like them and right away they start acting uppity. The heck with her now, though. She done lost me. Here she come now." Sam tucked his shirt in and stood up real straight.

Sure enough, Gloria was coming out of the house. Sam gave her a semi-hard look but she turned away from him. She was drinking one of those pineapple sodas she always seemed to be drinking and walked right past us.

"You done lost me, woman!" Sam called out after her. Gloria turned sharply and looked at him. "That's right, you done lost old Sam."

"Later for you, baby," she said. She said it so nasty, too. Then she turned and walked on down the street.

"She probably going some place to cry her eyes out," Sam suggested. "I'm going to buy her a present when I go downtown later, just to show her I really don't care. She can't hurt me, just herself."

"Yeah," I offered, "she's hitting the bottle already."

I told Cap what had happened and he told Binky who told Angel's sister, Maria, who met Clyde in the A & P and told him. So when Clyde came down the street and Sam started in his rap about Gloria, Clyde already knew. Cap had even big-mouthed about how Sam and me were going to ask Clyde to go to the dance. We told him we were sorry about that, and he said it was okay. He said that he was with his mother in the A & P when Maria told him, and later, when they got home, his mother told him he should go on to the dance.

"Years ago," she had told him, "down around New Orleans and Shreveport and places like that, people would march to a funeral and then come back and party. Oh, they'd march out to the burying ground— we didn't call them cemeteries—just as proper as you want. But, Lord, after we laid the body to rest they'd play up a storm on the way home, brass bands, mostly, and then they'd have a party. Somebody would always stay behind and cook up a mess of chicken or gumbo and we'd have a party. It wasn't no disrespect to the dead—just realizing that life was going to keep on going on. If crying was going to bring anybody back to life, then there wouldn't be any dead people. Your father worked too hard for you to throw away your life mourning for him. If he was here he'd tell you that. It's hard not thinking about somebody who passed on that you loved—it's hard, but life keeps going on."

"You want to go to the dance, Clyde?" I asked.

He just shrugged.

"Let's go across the street," Sam said. It was almost November and the shady side of the street was usually pretty cool.

"I guess I do," Clyde said as we parked ourselves on a stoop across from my building.

I saw my sister Sharon come out, look up and down the street until she spotted her girl friends, and then go tearing toward them. She'd made a lot of new friends in this neighborhood.

"Well, let's go." Sam was, as usual when he wasn't eating, retying his sneaker laces. "We can't win the twenty-five dollars unless we pick up some loose fox that can dance, but we might as well go."

"They upped the prize to fifty dollars," Clyde said.

"That's what Cap said," I told him.

"When they do that?" Sam asked, again pulling out his folded application. It was only twenty-five.

"Yesterday afternoon. Me, Cap, and Angel were over there shooting pool when they upped the prize. That's because so many people entered the contest. Cap and Angel entered. Angel's going to take his sister."

"Cap entered?" Sam jumped up.

Clyde nodded.

"That's why that dude didn't want you and Gloria entering! 'Cause he's the third best dancer after me and you, right?"

Clyde thought for a moment and then agreed. I wondered where I fit in. I mean, I was pretty smooth too, you know.

"That's why he didn't want you to enter. Go on and enter," Sam said to Clyde.

"Who am I going to take?"

"Borrow Angel's sister."

"Angel entered."

"How about Joan what's-her-name? You know, who lives over in the projects?"

"She dances too wild."

"How about Blondell? Hey, man, that's a bet. Blondell's outa sight!" Sam jumped up.

"Her mama got saved again."

"Which mean she can't go to dances for another six months. I swear I don't see how she keeps her dancing up, what with being saved half the time." Sam sat back down.

"You think Gloria will change her mind?"

"I don't know, man. Why don't you give her a call?"

"Hey, Stuff, go upstairs and give Gloria a call," Clyde said.

Call Gloria? Me?

In the first place, Gloria was older than me. In the second place, she could put other people down, and it was cool, and I even liked it, but when she put me down it hurt. So I didn't want to call her. But, on the other hand, I dug Clyde asking me to do it so I didn't know what to say. I didn't want to say I was afraid of Gloria, which I was a little bit, and I didn't want to say I didn't know what to say, which I didn't, but I didn't want to say no, either.

So I went upstairs and called Gloria, and her mother answered the phone. She said Gloria didn't feel well, but I could tell her mother was crying, too, and something was wrong. I came down and told Clyde and Sam that Gloria didn't feel well and didn't come to the phone.

"Too bad one of us ain't a girl," Sam said. "We could go with each other."

"Well, 116th Street never wins anything anyway. We lost the cleanest block award last year . . ." Clyde started.

". . . Yeah, and we lost the Catholic relays because Cap slipped in some dog mess . . ." Sam continued.

". . . And we lost the stoop ball contest when we had it in the bag because we showed up an hour late."

"I sure wish we could win this contest. Angel and Maria are okay but they ain't dynamite. Cap ain't bad but I hate to send third best out to do the best man's job," Sam concluded.

Anyway, what went down is that Angel and Maria dropped out because somebody got sick in Puerto Rico and they had to split on the morning of the contest. That left only Cap and his old lady in the contest from our block. Cap wanted the fifty dollars bad enough but he didn't really feel into a contest thing. What it was, I think, was that he got nervous when he heard that Carnation Charley from Morningside Avenue was entering the contest.

Now, you have to see Carnation Charley to believe him. He's about six feet tall or even more and he's got a real long neck. He's about my complexion and he wears his hair like he was born in the olden days or something—slicked down and all. Anyway, guess why they called him Carnation Charley? That's right, he always wore this carnation in his lapel. He had some nice vines, too. But—and this is the weird part—he could be decked out, see, I mean *decked out*, and he would wear sneakers. No lie. I mean, this guy could fall out in a cashmere suit, a silk shirt, a velvet vest, West Indian bracelets, an East African tiki, and Pro-Keds. I mean, can you dig it? But he'd have his carnation and that big smile and he'd be cool, see? And dance, oh, that cat could dance. He'd come to a dance with a game plan on a piece of paper. He'd take a look at his notes and get into his thing. He was the only guy I ever met that could jump straight up, the sweat popping off his brow, land in a perfect split, and jump up into the Funky Hustle without either missing a beat or changing the expression on his face.

But he had one fault. The way he danced, which was real good and everything, it seemed like work. He'd be sweating so bad that if he danced in one place for more than a minute there would be a puddle of sweat on the floor under where he stood. Anyway, that's the way it was. So Cap chickened out. He told Sam that he thought that he ("he" meaning Sam) should enter. Sam said he had already entered but he didn't have a girl. And then Sam had his big idea. Now, you see, when I think back on it, it seems kind of funny and everything, but I have to confess, at the time it seemed like a boss idea.

Sam and Clyde were going to enter the contest. Only, one of them was going to get decked out like a girl.

"You can be the woman, and I'll be the man and we can win this contest," Sam said. "Ain't nobody around going to beat us. And that's a f-a-c-t fact."

"How come I have to be the woman? You can be the woman, and I can be the guy."

"I got to be the guy," Sam said. "Because I can't be no woman."

"Why not?" asked Clyde.

"Because it messes with my image."

"And it messes with my image, too," Clyde countered.

"Anyway, I'm so manly that anybody looking at me could tell I was a man," Sam said.

We told Angel and Maria and it was decided that me, Angel, and Maria would decide who would be the girl and who would be the guy. Me and Angel figured the guy who was the most manly would be the guy and the other person would be the girl. Maria, Angel's sister, said the guy who was the most manly would be the girl 'cause it wouldn't bother him as much being the girl. Which made sense in a funny kind of way. Anyway, we had a manly contest to see who was the most manly between Clyde and Sam.

The contest was simple. Whoever did the manliest thing was going to be the woman and the other guy would be the man. We figured we had three votes and it couldn't be a tie. But that was before we considered Maria.

Sam and Clyde, me, Angel and Maria all met at Clyde's house. Sam was supposed to do his manly thing first.

"I am going to do fifty push-ups," Sam announced. "Every time I go down I'll go all the way down until my *mustache* touches the floor." When he said "mustache" he gave Clyde a look because Sam was the only one in the whole bunch who had even a little bit of a mustache.

"He got his mustache by having a transplant from under his arms," Clyde said.

"Yeah, baby," Sam said, "but match these fifty."

Sam then did fifty push-ups. I think he could have done more if he wanted to, too. Then it was Clyde's turn.

Clyde announced that he was going to take any torture that Sam could dish out. Torture!

"You're going to let him torture you?" Angel asked.

"Right," said Clyde, "and I'm going to take it without giving up."

"You got to be jiving, man. I'll put you through so many changes that you won't even remember your name. I'll put bamboo splinters under your eyelids and tap dance on your forehead. You might as well give it up, turkey, because you're going to be crying for mercy in the worse kind of way."

Clyde laid down on the floor and crossed his arms over his chest.

"Sock it to me, and see what a real man can take."

Sam looked down at Clyde on the floor and then went and got a fork, a knife, and a toothpick. I held my breath. I could just imagine what he was going to do. I imagined him sticking that toothpick under Clyde's eyelids and I shivered. Or I could imagine him sticking the fork into Clyde's stomach. But he didn't do anything. He couldn't hurt Clyde at all. Oh, he came near him with the fork and made a lot of little growling noises and what have you but he really couldn't hurt him. He got disgusted with himself.

"You win," he said. "I ain't even man enough to sock it to you."

Then we had a vote and me and Angel decided that Clyde was the winner because any dude that could stand torture had to be a real man. But that's when Maria got heavy.

"Not hurting his friend is more important to him than proving he's a man," Maria said, "and that makes him a real *person*. And in my book that's better than being a real *man*. Because being a real man is biology and what I'm talking about is living like people, dig? Not roles. This ain't MGM, this is 116th Street."

And so Angel and me got outvoted, one to two with the one being stronger than our two. And Clyde finally said that he'd be the girl anyway because he was the best-looking, and that's how they decided who was going to be who.

The morning of the big dance we all met in Clyde's house. His mother was going shopping and then she was going to work. She said she was going to have the groceries delivered and left fifty cents on the dresser as a tip for the delivery boy. Well, she shopped at Met Foods and they had a real young-looking white boy delivering the groceries and Clyde figured he would only give him a quarter so that was cool. You've probably figured out that everything that Clyde did was cool, right? Not quite, baby, not quite.

Okay, so we all gathered at Clyde's house. Cap had borrowed his half sister's wig and Sam had gotten a dress from his cousin and I'd copped some of my mother's cosmetics. So then we fixed up Clyde. I mean we fixed him up *good*. He had on a dress with half a tennis ball and some toilet tissue up front, some low platforms, some screw-on earrings, a wig, some lipstick, and a little bit of eye liner. Well, let me tell you, Clyde looked Boss. I mean, he was just so cute it was ridiculous. He started walking around acting real mannish because he felt self-conscious, but everyone was shocked because of how good he looked. They said he was the best-looking girl on the block. So he and Sam practiced some more and we told Clyde to get into a girl's thing.

"Hey, Clyde, why don't you wiggle your butt around a little?" I said.

"Because I don't want to wiggle my butt around, that's why!" he said.

"If you're going to be a girl you're going to be a girl. Wiggle a little!"

So he started wiggling a little. Just a little at first. And all the time he was looking around to see how we reacted. But when he saw that we were just looking at him like we wanted him to win the contest, he really started into a nice kind of wiggle. First it was a real exaggerated kind of wiggle, but then it kind of calmed down into a cute little thing that he did with his hips. Then Angel told him he wasn't doing it right.

"Do it like this, man." Angel walked around the room and started wiggling his butt and really looked like a girl, the way he walked, but Sam said that it wasn't the way he was wiggling his butt so much as the way he was moving his shoulders. Sam had a good eye for that kind of thing. And when Clyde started to move his shoulders just a little bit differently he really looked good.

Everybody thought he was really good and I had already decided how I could spend my part of the money. I figured to get ten dollars. I was going to give part of mine to charity, because that's the kind of guy I am. And with the other $9.75 I was going to buy two Stevie Wonder albums. Sam was going to buy a secondhand stopwatch to figure out just how fast he was, and Cap and Clyde hadn't decided yet. We had to give ten dollars to Cap's old lady, too, for being a technical consultant.

So the big night came. Carnation Charley was there, with this tall, long-legged girl. Sam and Clyde were there—we were calling him Claudette for the evening—and nobody else we knew. There were a few dances, when Sam and Clyde danced around just so they could get a feel of the floor. The floor was good, too. Not too dirty so you'd be slipping around and not too dead so you couldn't get any action.

Now Clyde wasn't looking too good but, then

again, he wasn't looking too bad. As a girl, I mean. Everything was cool, really, except me. I thought I was going to bust out laughing every time I looked over at Sam and Clyde. I mean Claudette. They were dancing pretty good and you could see Sam was starting to get into his thing. You could tell because when he got close to Claudette and started backing away he would kind of jerk his head from side to side and hunch his shoulders. Claudette was being blasé. I mean looking around the place like she just *knew* she was the most boss chick in the place. I tried to imagine Claudette as a real girl. I'd kind of look away and then look over casually and check her out. But then I'd see Sam twisting and going into his thing and I'd crack up. But I kept my hand over my mouth so it didn't look too bad. Then when I had a real fit of laughing I'd point to Carnation Charley.

The funny thing about it is that Carnation Charley was checking out Sam and Claudette, too. First he'd sneak a little peek from the corner of his eye, and then when they weren't looking in his direction he'd practically stop and peel his eyeballs back to get a good look. You see, Carnation Charley knew that Fast Sam could really dance. I guess he was saying to himself something like "Hey, look, there's Fast Sam with a cool-looking chick." Now that was important, to have a girl that could dance, too. A lot of guys dance so far away from their partners, doing all this acrobatic stuff, that they could be dancing with the jukebox.

But the real groovy dancers, like Carnation Charley and Fast Sam and Clyde (when he wasn't being Claudette, which was all of the time except that night) danced close to their partners and acted as if they really enjoyed dancing. Even Carnation Charley, who would be sweating and carrying on until his suit got wet under the arms clear through his shirt, would manage to smile at his partner every once in a while.

Then the announcer, who was Mr. Reese, the center's athletic coach, turned off the record player and said it was time for the dance contest. Then he went around and gave everybody a number. Your partner and you would both have the same number, see? And the announcer would tell people to sit down until there was just one couple on the floor. Okay, now there was going to be two rounds to the contest. The first round was going to have a Jackson Five tape which they had made about four minutes long, and the second round was going to have a fast number by Al Green, which was really dynamite. Sam and Claudette had number thirty-seven and Carnation Charley had number twenty-eight. The announcer looked at everybody for a long time and then called out:

"Let's party!"

And the dance was on. Do you hear? The dance was ON! Everybody on the floor was looking like dynamite. Going through their numbers, dig? Sometimes they were doing the same thing. The guy would turn left and the girl would turn right and you could see that they had been practicing for some time. Then everybody had their own little number. Some little step that nobody had seen before or something. See, if you threw a step on them that nobody had seen before, everybody would have to say, "Wow! That guy's got a new step!" And then they'd realize they'd have to come up with something to match it. But you had practiced yours and they had to make theirs up right on the spot and then try to get it coordinated with the girl. But in the Jackson Five number nobody was doing too much. I mean, there were a few steps that I hadn't exactly seen but they were really only a little different from ones I had seen. Also, Carnation Charley had pulled a few moves during the warm-up where he fell back and caught himself on one hand and then came back up again. It looked okay and Sam thought that when they got to the final round he was going to try it out. But Sam and Claudette had a little something, too. They had this move—get this—where Claudette leaned all the way back and swung around three times and Sam leaned back and swung around three times, then Claudette leaned forward and swung around once while Sam swung his leg over Claudette's head. I had seen them do it in Clyde's living room and it was *bad*.

Anyway the dance is going on and the announcer starts calling out numbers. When he calls your number he says, "Hey, hey, hey, let's give a big hand to number so-and-so." And then everybody gives you this

big hand and you sit down because you've been eliminated.

"Hey, hey, hey, let's give a big hand to number
fourteen!" And fourteen, this short fat little guy,
stopped dancing on a dime. Whomp! The cat was
stone still and he gave the announcer an evil look that
would make water run backwards. Then he strutted
on off. The announcer gave a few more numbers and
the floor started to clear out a little.

Now when the floor is crowded you can get by. But
when there's not too many people on the dance floor
you have to let it hang out. Okay. The pace is picking
up. The music's getting good and everybody around
the floor is doing their own little move as the dancers
are doing their thing. The announcer keeps calling out
numbers and the floor's getting thinner and thinner.
But the record is almost coming to an end, too. So
everybody had to hang on in there a little longer.
Finally there were about nine couples on the floor and
about a half a minute to go. And the announcer went
into his hey, hey, hey bit. Well, let me tell you what
happens. When the announcer starts his hey, hey, hey
he already knows what couple he's going to sit down.
But the couple doesn't know it, so everytime he gets
into a hey, hey, hey the dance gets a little more fran-
tic. Because you throw out your best move so it won't
be you that has to sit down. Not only that, people
from the sidelines start yelling things out too. Things
like:

"Hey, sit number nine down. He can't dance!"

"Number thirty-one must be a cripple. Either that or his shoes are on the wrong feet!"

Well, like I said, there were about nine couples on the floor and the first round was almost over. The announcer went into his hey, hey, hey and three things happened. Carnation Charley went into his fall back, and two other couples bumped into each other and both of the guys fell. When Carnation Charley sees this he gets nervous and he comes up and falls back again, only this time he don't catch himself right and he hurts his wrist. You look at this guy and you know he has hurt his wrist. His wrist hurts so bad he wants to cry. But he keeps dancing. I mean Carnation Charley has heart. Anyway, the announcer calls the numbers of both the guys that fell and they stalk off the floor mad as anything. I don't think they were that good but their ladies were really outa sight. It's always some guy who's not into much that gets mad first.

Then there was the intermission and Sam and Claudette come over and sit with me. Some other people came over, but Sam said that Claudette wasn't feeling too well and please not to crowd her. So they left. I told Sam about how I thought Carnation Charley had hurt himself and Sam said that he knew. He heard him grunt when he hit the floor the second time. We looked over to where the Carnation was sitting and he looked over at us and gave us this big smile. He looked like a crocodile with a toothache.

His old lady was rubbing his wrist and trying to get it back together again but I knew it was too late. When the announcer called the contestants back onto the floor Carnation Charley went out like an old gunfighter who knew his time had come.

The music started again and Al Green, with his high voice and funky self, starts singing and grooving and the dancing gets serious. All the lames are off the floor and the D-A-N-C-E-R-S are on the floor. Sam was really getting into his thing and he looked like the best. Carnation Charley wasn't slouching either— he was just about perfect. The music played on and the dancers danced on. Somebody on the sideline bet seventy-five cents on Carnation Charley and somebody else bet fifty cents on Sam and Claudette. Two more numbers were called. There were four couples left on the floor.

Now, with four couples on the floor and the floor getting a bit slippery you had to be careful, and this is where Carnation Charley's sneakers came in. He wasn't about to slip in them sneakers. I was a little worried. Then the announcer called another number. Sam and Claudette, Carnation Charley and his woman, and this Puerto Rican couple were still on the floor. I knew the Puerto Rican couple didn't have a chance. They were good, real good, but they just weren't fancy enough. Sure enough, after a few minutes the announcer called their number and they had to sit down. Everybody gave them a real big hand.

It lasted almost a minute. Then there was only about a minute left and Carnation Charley went into his thing. He did his fallback thing, but instead of falling back to the floor where he would hurt his wrist he just leaned all the way back and touched his heels and came up again. But he did it good. I mean the guy was really going. Everyone started clapping and my heart jumped into my throat. Then Sam and Clyde started doing their thing. They did their lean back and spin and it was outa sight, too. Then they did it again, only this time they did it twice in a row without stopping, and the people started clapping again, but this time for Sam and Clyde, I mean Claudette. Then they went into a third time. But this time they both went around two times, froze for about four beats and then finished it with Sam swinging his leg over Claudette's head, dropping into a modified split, then he came up, they both spun again, this time slower, went through the whole routine again *slower* until Sam hit his modified split and then started the whole thing again *even slower.* And cool. Oh, it was so cool. They were slowing down and finishing with the music and everybody started yelling and clapping and it was all over. The announcer called out "Hey, hey, hey, let's give a big hand to Carnation Charley." Carnation Charley had to sit down. Sam and Clyde had won the money! I felt so good I didn't know what to do with myself. Carnation Charley came over to Sam and gave him five and then five more on the black hand side and then some more palm. That was really together, seeing how he had lost and everything. It had been a great contest and a great win.

The story would have ended there except for the victory dance. The guy who won had to dance with the first girl eliminated and the girl who won had to dance with the first guy eliminated. They played a slow Roberta Flack side. In Sam's case that was cool because he was too tired to dance fast any more. So he takes this chick onto the floor and starts dancing with her. He had already gave me the money to hold and he was feeling all right. And Clyde was dancing with this guy and everybody drifted onto the floor and started dancing. It was a slow number—Roberta Flack does a lot of slow numbers that are hard to dance to—and they turned the lights down a little. Not way down like in a grind-em-up but just kind of dim. Now get this, this clown that Clyde is dancing with wants to dance close. Can you dig it? He keeps pushing and Clyde keeps backing away. And he keeps trying to dance close enough for a cheap thrill. So Clyde kind of murmurs uh-uhn to this guy, but he don't take no for an answer. Now Clyde can't get engaged in any heavy conversation with this dude because he's going to recognize that Clyde ain't Claudette. So Clyde is just backing away and this guy keeps moving on forward. I guess he must have figured that Clyde was just bashful or something. And this was a weird-looking dude, too. Tall and skinny with a real stupid grin. Anyway he keeps pushing up against Clyde and finally Clyde stops and gives him a little poke in the ribs. Then this guy rubs his hand on Clyde's side and starts talking about how he was getting all excited and everything and didn't Clyde want to give him a little soul kiss. Clyde was just about to lay another uh-uhn on the dude when the guy suddenly lifts Clyde's chin and sticks his tongue in Clyde's mouth in a soul kiss. That was when Clyde took off his wig and punched the dude in the mouth. Man, the place cracked up entirely. They put the bright lights back on suddenly and there was Clyde, the wig on the floor behind him, wailing on this dude. The announcer like to have had a fit. Sam didn't say a word, he just came over to me, took the money out of my hand and went over and gave it to Carnation Charley. Then me and him pulled Clyde out of the place, while the guy Clyde was dancing with sat in the middle of the floor, holding his jaw and wondering what the heck had happened.

the good people

4 *Sometimes things can happen and even though* the thing that happens is bad you don't mind so much because no one knows about it except you. It's like having on raggedy underwear. You don't really feel cool having it on, but you don't feel nearly as bad as if you knew somebody else knew. If you were in school, for example, and somebody knew you had on raggedy underwear you'd spend all day thinking that person was thinking about you and your raggedy underwear. And if that person went up to another person and started talking so that you couldn't hear what they were saying, well, right away you'd be thinking that they were talking about you. You might even think your underwear was showing through your clothes or something.

Everybody has had on raggedy underwear or something like that that they really didn't want anybody to find out about. Take Little Petey Johnson, for example. Now Little Petey was a smart guy and was supposed to graduate from Lane about a year ago. So it's time for him to graduate and he doesn't show up. The music is going and everybody is coming down the aisle and still he don't show. A lot of guys didn't graduate and naturally they weren't in the ceremony, but the ones that did graduate were pretty happy with themselves. They were looking for Petey because he was in the graduation group. After all the diplomas were given out, a few medals and a lot of speeches, everybody went outside of the theater and started signing each other's book. They held the ceremony in a theater instead of the school auditorium.

Then somebody spots Little Petey Johnson.

He was standing on a stoop across the street drinking a Coca-Cola. They went over and asked him why he hadn't come to the graduation and he said that it was just a jive ceremony and he was tired of jive ceremonies. Now that was really heavy because the ceremony might have been jive but you were still graduating from high school. Later we learned the real reason why Petey hadn't shown up. Everybody had been talking about how sharp they were going to be in their blue suits, which all the boys were going to wear. And Petey just couldn't get the money together for a new suit and he didn't want to be the only one different. He felt bad about not coming to the graduation but I guess he would have felt worse if everybody knew that he couldn't afford the suit.

Anyway, the same thing happened to Gloria. When me, Clyde, and Sam were telling everybody about the dance and how Sam and Clyde almost won, everybody cracked up except Gloria. Gloria had been acting funny for a while but nobody knew why. Sometimes she would come and sit on the stoop with us for a while, but just for a short time, as if she had to do it to be respectable or something. You could see that she wasn't really enjoying it or anything.

Then one day we were all sitting on the stoop, me, Gloria, Clyde, Sam, Binky, Cap, Maria, and this girl named Debbie. When all of a sudden we hear all this noise and scuffling in the hallway. We all turned to look and made a space on the stoop so whoever it was could pass if they were leaving. All of a sudden Gloria's father comes out with a suitcase and you could see that he was really mad. And her mother was right after him and she was mad too. She was wearing a house dress with an apron.

"If I *ever* see you again—" Gloria's mother was half talking and half crying. "If I *ever* lay eyes on you again it'll be too soon!"

"You don't have to worry none about me coming back!" Mr. Chisholm said. "You don't have to worry about me coming back. Why don't you go on back upstairs and polish your nails again, Miss Queen!"

Well, they kept on shouting at each other for what seemed a long time, with her saying that she hated him and he saying that he never wanted to be with her in the first place and things like that. Then Mrs. Chisholm pushed right up against him and started talking real fast and half crying, and suddenly Mr. Chisholm hit her. He didn't punch her but he slapped her as hard as I've seen anybody get slapped. He slapped her so hard that everybody on the stoop jumped. Really. I took a look at Gloria and the tears were running down her face and she really looked miserable. Mrs. Chisholm just slowly went down. Not so much from being slapped but from everything—the arguing, the crying, and the slap. She just took a couple of deep breaths and sunk to the sidewalk. I didn't know what to do—none of us did, I guess. Mr. Chisholm picked up his suitcase and started to walk away when Gloria suddenly jumped up and ran after him and hit him on the back. He whirled around like he was going to punch her out, but when he saw it was Gloria he just kind of pushed her away. And she hit him again and again and started screaming that she hated him, just like her mother did. He just kind of kept his hands in front of him so she couldn't get at him and kept backing away. Then Gloria looked back to where her mother was and took a couple of steps toward her and then looked at her father and then back at her mother. It was as if she didn't know what to do. She turned and started back toward her mother but she stopped one more time and called after her father. Her voice was all cracked up and so full of crying that it was hard to understand what she was saying except she said it over and over again.

"Daddy, please don't go! Daddy, please don't go! Daddy, please don't go. . . ." She kept saying it over and over even though she wasn't saying it nearly loud enough for him to hear it. And then she just turned away when she couldn't see him any more and went back and helped her mother up. And together they went into the house and she was still saying it, in this tiny little voice. "Daddy, please don't go."

Clyde looked at me and I looked at him and we both looked at Sam. Sam looked terrible and I felt about as bad for him as I felt for Gloria. Almost, anyway.

"Hey, man, maybe you can check her out later," Clyde said to Sam, giving his knee a little punch. "Let her get it out of her system a little and then maybe give her a call later or tomorrow morning."

"That's why she didn't want to go to the dance before. I spoke to her for about a hot minute yesterday and she said things weren't going down too good between her folks." Sam shrugged his shoulders. "Every time I even think that girl feels bad I feel bad."

"What did you say when she said her folks weren't getting along too good?" Clyde asked.

"I didn't know what to say," Sam said, "I just told her that as far as I was concerned me and her were still tight."

"She go for that?" Clyde asked.

"Yeah." Sam smiled a sheepish smile. "I'll call her later."

"It's bad when your folks don't make it," Clyde said. "You don't know what to do."

"At least we can talk about it some," Sam said.

"'Cause it ain't our folks," Clyde said. "A lot of times things happen and you can see the problem but you can't help it."

"Nothing you can do about that," I said.

"Maybe not, maybe yes," Clyde said. There was a faraway look in his eyes.

We didn't see Gloria for some time and then one day when we were down at the center cleaning it up we got some news about her. (We had to clean the center twice a week for an entire month after the dance because of them catching Clyde dressed up like a girl.) Anyway, Maria had went down to the welfare office with a friend of hers and she said that she saw Gloria and her mother in the new-application section of the welfare office. We said that we hadn't seen Gloria in about a month. Sam wanted to ask some more questions, like how Gloria was acting—was she crying or anything—but Clyde told us to get on with the cleaning and let's get out of the center. I got the feeling he was telling us to shut up. After we finished cleaning, me and Clyde and Sam went over to Freddie's restaurant and sat in a booth and had coffee. Clyde liked to do that and so did Sam. I hated coffee

but I dug sitting in the booth drinking it. I thought
it was pretty cool at the time.

"How come you didn't let me ask about Gloria,
man?" Sam said, putting his fourth spoonful of sugar
in his coffee. "After all, she is one of the group."

"Why did you want to know about her?" Clyde
said, in this real cool voice. That's one thing about
Clyde. When he had something really heavy to lay
on you he always came up with this cool voice and
you just knew you were going to be zonked. Then
he'd ask you a question and you knew you weren't
going to get the answer right. Sam looks at me and
I looked back at Sam, trying to be cool like Clyde
did, so he would think I knew what Clyde was thinking.

"What you mean, why did I want to know about
her?" Sam said, stalling for time.

"Just what I said," Clyde came back.

"Well, I just wanted to know what happened, that's
all. I mean, that's natural, right?" Sam looked at me.
That sounded pretty good to me so I nodded. When
I did this he went on talking. "When you know somebody it's natural that you should want to know what
they're doing, see. There ain't no particular reason,
you just naturally want to know." Sam slurped down
some coffee and that made the waitress look over at
us and shake her head.

"But that's the problem," Clyde said. "You said
that Gloria is part of the group. Then there should

be a special reason. There should be a special reason for us to find out what's happening to her."

"That's what I said. Only you're saying it's special and I'm saying it's natural. Same difference, man." Sam slurped his coffee again and I looked over at the waitress and she shook her head again.

"No, what I'm saying is that we shouldn't get into her business at all unless we're going to try to help her. I mean, if all we're going to do about her being down at the welfare office is *use* it as something to talk about and pass the time of day, well, why bother? We can talk about the moon or the World Series or anything."

"You mean," I said, thinking I was into something, "that we ought to take up a collection for her?"

Clyde didn't say anything. He just turned real slow and gave me a look. For a young dude he had a cutting look, I want to tell you.

"What we can do," Clyde said, mercifully looking back to Sam, "is to let her know that we care. You know, we haven't seen Gloria in a while but we really haven't made an effort to either."

That was right. Even her girl friend, this girl everybody called BB but whose real name was Karen, hadn't been around to see her. Mostly because Gloria just wasn't as easy to get along with as she had been before. BB was saying that Gloria was being defensive.

"So what we gonna do. Bust on up to her house and say things to her?" Sam asked. "You going to do the talking?"

"You can do the talking if you want to," said Clyde.

"I wouldn't know what to say."

"I don't think it makes that much difference really. If you go up and she sees what we're trying to do she'll understand. And anyway, when my father died you came up and talked to me. That's what gave me the idea really." Clyde looked right at Sam and Sam kind of smiled.

"Well, we got to stick together," Sam said, pleased that Clyde had said it was his idea.

"You know, I don't know about other kids, but, dig, we got a lot of problems. You know, my father died. Gloria's going through this thing."

"I don't have any problems," I said.

"You know what else you don't have, Stuff?" Sam asked.

"What?"

"Mirrors. Because if you had yourself a mirror and looked into it you'd see that you had a problem. I mean, if your face was your only fortune you'd be on welfare."

"You think he could use a face lift?" Clyde asked. I knew they were just getting on me because I was younger than they were. Sometimes when they had nothing else to do they'd get on me just to pass the time.

"No, I don't think he can use a face lift. He could use a face drop. Maybe they could drop it somewhere around his chest so his shirt would cover it up."

"Aw, man."

"So come on. Let's go over to Gloria's house now," Sam said, finishing his coffee with one last slurp.

"Who's going to do the talking?" Clyde asked.

"You," Sam said.

"What will I say?"

"What will you say? Hey, look, you were the one that said that it didn't matter what we said. Right, Stuff? Didn't he just . . ."

"I said that, but we ought to have something definite to say, too. We just can't walk in and start stuttering around. I mean, I don't know . . . let me think about it until tomorrow. Okay?"

"Okay," Sam said. It was okay with me too because I had to get home by nine and it was already five past nine.

The next day we were all supposed to meet at three thirty, but I couldn't get there until four because my mother called from her job and said that I had to clean the bathroom before I left the house because I had got home late the night before. I asked her if I could clean it for just ten minutes because I was only ten minutes late but she said no. And that if I didn't do a good job I'd have to answer to my father. And that's a pain, you know. Because he always comes up with these long lectures about how lucky I am and how hard he had it as a boy and all that kind of thing. And while he goes through all of this lecture bit I'm supposed to sit there and look like I'm really interested when the only thing I'm really interested in is his finishing.

Anyway, I start cleaning the bathroom as fast as I can, see, when Sharon comes in with four of her friends. And don't you know, they all have to go to the bathroom. Well, I tell them that they can't use the bathroom and one of them says she really has to go.

"Tough titty," I said.

"I'm going to tell Mama on you and you're going to get it." Sharon waved her finger in my face (which she knew I really hated).

"How would you like your teeth knocked out?"

"And I'm going to tell Mama that you said you were going to knock my teeth out, too."

"I don't even care."

"*And* I'm going to tell her that you said that you don't care if she knows it or not."

"I didn't say that. I said that I didn't care what you told her," I said.

I didn't say anything else, just closed the bathroom door.

"You open this door right now, Francis!" she said. And before I had a chance to even think about it she opened the door herself. "Edith has to use the bathroom and she's going to use it because this is my house as well as yours and my friends have just as much right to go to the bathroom as your friends and Mama's going to hear about this whole incident."

"Well, I'm not leaving. If she wants to use the bathroom with me in here she's welcome to it!"

You know what she called me then? A pervert. Only she said it pre-vert.

"You pre-vert!"

Now where did she learn a word like that? Anyway she gets on the phone to Mama's job and I know I'm going to lose this fight. I wanted to grab the phone from her, but I knew she'd just tell Mama that when Mama got home. She told Mama everything and then some.

"Mama, this is Sharon." Can you believe she was crying? "I came home with three of my girl friends because you said that I could always bring my girl friends to the house instead of hanging around in the streets and getting into trouble and one of them had to go to the bathroom real bad and she's an older girl almost eleven years old and may have her period any minute now and Francis won't let them use the bathroom and he said if I called you he was going to beat me up and knock out my teeth and he said that he didn't care if you knew it or not and he said a dirty word which I wouldn't even repeat!"

The next thing I knew I was on the phone and Mama was saying that I had to let them use the bathroom and why couldn't I be a gentleman for just once in my life. And she asked me what word I said and I said I didn't remember the word. She said she would speak to me when she got home. That was all. She must have forgot to tell me that I couldn't go out, which is what she usually did when I did something wrong. So then all of Sharon's girl friends went to the bathroom. Naturally, Sharon had to go too and

stay an extra-long time. But then the first girl that
went said that she had to go again! Twice! I said,
"How can you go to the bathroom twice like that?"
But then Sharon said that I wasn't supposed to ask
girls questions like that.

I finally got to the meeting at four o'clock. We met
at Clyde's house and Clyde said that he pretty much
knew what he was going to say. So we all went to
Gloria's house and her mother was home. So we sat
around for a while and then her mother said that she
had to go out and get some air.

"I know when I'm in the way," she said. "You want
me to bring anything back?"

"No, thanks," Gloria said.

After her mother left, Sam stood up and squared
his shoulders off. "Gloria," he said, "we've been thinking about this and that, you know. About what's going
on in the community. And we've been talking a lot
about it and we decided . . ." Sam looked at me and
Clyde. ". . . We decided that Clyde has something
to say." Sam sat down just as the doorbell rang. Gloria
looked at Sam and then at Clyde and then answered
the doorbell. It was Maria, BB, and Angel.

"Hey, you guys want to go over and shoot some
baskets?" Angel asked. He couldn't really play basketball very well but he loved it.

"Come on in, man, we got a meeting going on,"
Sam said.

So everybody came in and sat around. BB and

Angel were looking real serious and Gloria was looking suspicious.

"This is a little like a speech," Clyde said, "but it's something I really feel. I think it's important to me and I hope it's important to everybody else. Well, here goes. A lot of us have problems and sometimes it's hard to get around them. Some things you just can't do anything about. And when that happens you feel bad and you feel little. Not little, but alone. Because you don't want anyone knowing how you feel because it's so hard to tell people how you feel sometimes. When my father died, for example, I really felt bad and so did Kitty. Kitty should be up here."

"You want me to go get her?" BB asked.

"No, I'll tell her about it later. Anyway I've been thinking about this a lot. And I thought that we could form a club of some kind. And the purpose of the club would be to protect each other, not from fighting and that kind of thing but just from being alone when things get messed up. Sam came up when I was feeling real bad, and I could talk to him and he liked me so it helped. See, he liked me before, and I knew that he did, but he came up and talked with me when I needed some talking to. I don't know if I would have did the same for him. Not that I don't like Sam but I don't know if I would have thought about it. That was the cool thing. He *thought* about it. And when I think about him coming up and saying the things he did, real helpful things, it was good but it wasn't as good as thinking about the fact that if I need him again he'll be there, because that's the kind of guy he is. And, really, that's the kind of people most of us are. And if we kind of get together and decide that we're going to like each other—not like each other, but—"

"Care for each other," BB said.

"Dig it, *care* for each other, then we'll always know that we have each other to fall back on. We can do it as just friends, but if we agree to do it *before* things go wrong, then we'll know that we have something else."

"What's that?" Angel asked.

"Somebody who cares for us all the time. Whether things are right or wrong. So when things go wrong we don't have to go around looking for someone who'll like us and understand what we're all about. We'll have people we can turn to. We'll have each other. And we should be able to dig on each other's problems."

"Yeah, and we always get the same kind of problems. Somebody is sad because they don't have any money or something like that or they got family trouble or school trouble," Angel said. "Everybody in this whole neighborhood gets just about the same kind of problems."

"Who's going to be in the club?" Gloria asked.

"Whoever feels they can dig us as we are," said Clyde. "I don't think we should put anybody down

or keep them out of the club if they can be down-
to-earth and be like us. They don't even have to like
everybody in the club. Just know that nobody's any
different."

"I'm all for it," Sam said.

"Me too," I added.

"Okay for me and Maria," Angel said.

"Okay for me on my *own*," Maria said.

"Okay." Gloria.

BB nodded.

"We gonna give ourselves a name?" Sam asked.

"What do you think?" Clyde asked.

Everybody thought we should have a name.

"How about the Bloody Skulls?" Sam asked.

"Now how would we look with a name like the
Bloody Skulls?" Clyde asked.

"Then how about the Golden Imperial Knights?"

"How about the Golden Imperial Margarines?"

"Come on, BB, I'm being serious." Sam was seri-
ously frowning. "If you got a club you have to have
a dynamite name."

"How about jackets?" Angel asked.

"He's not talking about that kind of club!" Maria
snapped. "I mean, we're not going to be a bopping
club or anything. This is like a social club. Not even
that, a community club."

"We don't even have to have a name if we don't
want," Clyde suggested. "Names and jackets are
okay—I'm not really against them—but that's not
really what we're all about."

"Let's call ourselves the Good People," BB suggested.

"That's corny," I said.

"I'm corny." BB gave me a look. "We're talking about being corny and caring for each other, so let's be corny all the way. I care for all of you, and I'm not ashamed of it, you know. I don't mind being called the Good People and I don't care if anyone else in the world thinks it's corny. If I get some people in my corner, some people who are going to care for me, I don't care what anybody else thinks."

"Then that's who we are. The Good People," Maria said.

"At least let's make it the 116th Street Good People," Sam said.

"You got it, man," Angel said.

"Okay." Clyde.

"Okay." Gloria.

"And when we have problems, we'll talk about them?" Clyde asked.

Everybody agreed. I could see that everyone was happy with the club, too.

"You mean like our fathers being dead?" Gloria asked.

Clyde looked up at her and then toward BB. BB looked down real quick.

"I didn't know your father was dead, Gloria," Clyde said.

"He's dead," Gloria said.

"How did he die?" Clyde asked.

"He got hit by a truck."

"Oh. When did that happen?"

"About a month ago."

I looked at Clyde and he looked away from me. I wanted to say something to Gloria, to tell her that Clyde and I would understand and that she didn't have to lie to us. I thought of our agreement—that we agreed to help each other—and I realized that we had formed a club to help each other and maybe we should have formed one to agree to *accept* help from each other.

Clyde didn't believe Gloria, I knew. I knew that Gloria's father was alive just a few days ago. Gloria's eyes glistened over. Clyde didn't say anything. We just sat around for a while longer, and then Angel said he was going out to the stoop. Maria went with him and Sam and BB and me. I thought that Clyde was going to stay and talk with Gloria, but we weren't on the steps more than a minute when he came and sat with us. He started talking about this and that and asked me how I was doing on the sax. I said okay. I never did understand how people could talk about things they weren't thinking about.

Gloria came out just as her mother came up. Her mother had bought a six pack of sodas and she passed them out. Then she went on inside.

"He lost his job," Gloria said to us.

"Who?"

"My father. He come home one day and said he didn't want any supper and then he sat in the living room and talked about how his company had moved down South and how he had to look for another job and he was wondering what kinds of things he wanted to get into and everything. Then he started looking around for a job and he couldn't find nothing. And when he came home you couldn't talk to him or anything. Then one day Mama and I came home and we were jiving around and everything and started fixing dinner—I love it when she lets me do the dinner—well, then we hear this crying from the living room. At first we were real scared because the living room was dark. Then we got up enough nerve to turn on the lamp, and it was my father. He had been drinking and then he was crying. He hadn't found a job and it was really getting to him, you know. After that he kept arguing with Mama until he started talking about leaving.

"He doesn't read too well, so it's really hard for him to get a good job. He's smart enough in a street kind of way but he's not really into books and that kind of thing. Then they had this big fight and everything. They were yelling at each other and cursing and going on. I really hate him for hitting her. You know, I just hate him for that." Gloria was quiet for a long minute. "Or maybe I don't. Maybe I just hate that he had to do it that way. I hope he's all right. He didn't take his winter coat. Mama says she doesn't know how he's going to get along without his winter coat."

"You think he's going to come back?" Angel asked.

"Yeah, I think so," Gloria said, smiling through her tears. "That's what makes it not so bad. He's okay for a cat that's not too heavy."

"I think he'll be back," BB said.

"BB, you'll always think the right thing as long as you live, girl," Gloria said, sniffling a little. "You got a big heart for a young girl. I really mean that, too."

"Hey, Gloria!" Sam.

"What you want, main man?"

"How come you decided to come out to the stoop with us?"

"Heard there was a jive club down here called the 116th Street Good People. Figured I'd check them out."

Then we started in to laughing and playing around. If somebody came around and looked at us they'd probably think we were just being stupid, but the real thing was that we felt good. We had something real close and we were glad about it. It filled me up with so much gladness that laughing and crying were almost the same thing. It was a good night, maybe one of my best nights ever.

trombones and colleges

5 *It was a dark day when we got our report cards.* The sky was full of gray clouds and it was sprinkling rain. I was over to Clyde's house and Gloria and Kitty were there. Sam probably would have been there too, only he had got a two-week job in the afternoons helping out at Freddie's. Actually he only did it so that his mother would let him be on the track team again. Sam and his mother had this little system going. He would do something good-doing and she'd let him do something that he wanted to.

Clyde's report card was on the kitchen table and we all sat around it like it was some kind of a big important document. I had got a pretty good report card and had wanted to show it off but I knew it wasn't the time. Clyde pushed the card toward me and I read it. He had all satisfactory remarks on the side labeled Personal Traits and Behavior. He had also received B's in music and art appreciation. But everything else was either a C or a D except mathematics. His mathematics mark was a big red F that had been circled. I don't know why they had to circle the F when it was the only red mark on the card. In the Teacher's Comments section someone had written that Clyde had "little ability to handle an academic program."

"A little ability is better than none," I said. No one said anything so I figured it probably wasn't the right time to try to cheer Clyde up.

I knew all about his switching from a commercial program to an academic program, but I really hadn't thought he'd have any trouble.

"I saw the grade adviser today. He said I should switch back to the commercial program." Clyde looked like he'd start crying any minute. His eyes were red and his voice was shaky. "He said that I had to take mathematics over and if I failed again or failed another required subject I couldn't graduate. The way it is now I'm going to have to finish up in the summer because I switched over."

"I think you can pass it if you really want to," Kitty said. Clyde's sister was so pretty I couldn't even look at her. If I did I started feeling funny and couldn't talk right. Sometimes I daydreamed about marrying her.

Just then Clyde's mother came in and he gave a quick look at Kitty.

"Hi, young ladies and young gentlemen." Mrs. Jones was a kind of heavy woman but she was pretty, too. You could tell she was Kitty's mother if you looked close. She put her package down and started taking things out. "I heard you people talking when I first came in. By the way you hushed up I guess you don't want me to hear what you were talking about. I'll be out of your way in a minute, soon as I put the frozen foods in the refrigerator."

"I got my report card today," Clyde said. His mother stopped taking the food out and turned toward us. Clyde pushed the report card about two inches toward her. She really didn't even have to look at the card to know that it was bad. She could have told that just by looking at Clyde. But she picked it up and looked at it a long time. First she looked at one side and then the other and then back at the first side again.

"What they say around the school?" she asked, still looking at the card.

"They said I should drop the academic course and go back to the other one." I could hardly hear Clyde, he spoke so low.

"Well, what you going to do, young man?" She looked up at Clyde and Clyde looked up at her and there were tears in his eyes and I almost started crying. I can't stand to see my friends cry. "What are you going to do, Mr. Jones?"

"I'm—I'm going to keep the academic course," Clyde said.

"You think it's going to be any easier this time?"
Mrs. Jones asked.

"No."

"Things ain't always easy. Lord knows that things
ain't always easy." For a minute there was a faraway
look in her eyes, but then her face turned into a big
smile. "You're just like your father, boy. That man
never would give up on anything he really wanted.
Did I ever tell you the time he was trying to learn
to play the trombone?"

"No." Clyde still had tears in his eyes but he was
smiling, too. Suddenly everybody was happy. It was
like seeing a rainbow when it was still raining.

"Well, we were living over across from St. Nicholas
Park in this little rooming house. Your father was
working on a job down on Varick Street that made
transformers or some such nonsense—anyway, he
comes home one day with this long package all
wrapped up in brown paper. He walks in and sits it
in the corner and doesn't say boo about what's in the
bag. So at first I don't say anything either, and then
I finally asks him what he's got in the bag, and he
says, 'What bag?' Now this thing is about four feet
long if it's an inch and he's asking *what* bag." Mrs.
Jones wiped the crumbs from Gloria's end of the table
with a quick swipe of the dish cloth, leaving a swirling
pattern of tiny bubbles. Gloria tore off a paper towel
and wiped the area dry.

"Now I look over at him and he's trying to be

nonchalant. Sitting there, a grown man, and big as
he wants to be and looking for all the world like
somebody's misplaced son. So I says, 'The bag in the
corner.' And he says, 'Oh, that's a trombone I'm taking back to the pawn shop tomorrow.' Well, I naturally ask him what he's doing with it in the first place,
and he says he got carried away and bought it but
he realized that we really didn't have the thirty-five
dollars to spend on foolishness and so he'd take it
back the next day. And all the time he's sitting there
scratching his chin and rubbing his nose and trying
to peek over at me to see how I felt about it. I just
told him that I guess he knew what was best. Only
the next day he forgot to take it back, and the next
day he forgot to take it back, and finally I broke down
and told him why didn't he keep it. He said he would
if I thought he should.

"So he unwraps this thing and he was just as happy
with it as he could be until he tried to get a tune
out of it. He couldn't get a sound out of it at first,
but then he started oomping and woomping with the
thing as best he could. He worked at it and worked
at it and you could see he was getting disgusted. I
think he was just about to give it up when the lady
who lived under us came upstairs and started com-
plaining about the noise. It kept her Napoleon awake,
she said. Napoleon was a dog. Little ugly thing, too.
She said your father couldn't play, anyway.

"Well, what did she say that for? That man played

that thing day and night. He worked so hard at that thing that his lips were too sore for him to talk right sometime. But he got the hang of it."

"I never remembered Pop playing a trombone," said Clyde.

"Well, your father had a streak in him that made him stick to a thing," she said, pouring some rice into a colander to wash it off, "but every year his goals got bigger and bigger and he had to put some things down so that he could get to others. That old trombone is still around here some place. Probably in one of them boxes under Kitty's bed. Now, you children, excuse me, young ladies and gentlemen, get on out of here and let me finish supper."

We all went into Clyde's living room.

"That was my mom's good-doing speech," Clyde said. "She gets into talking about what a great guy my father was and how I was like him and whatnot."

"You supposed to be like your father," Sam said. "He was the one that raised you, right?"

"She wants me to be like him, and I want to be like him, too, I guess. She wants me to keep on trying with the academic thing."

"What you want to do," Sam asked, "give it up?"

"No. Not really. I guess I want people like my mother to keep on telling me that I ought to do it, really. Especially when somebody tells me I can't do it."

"Boy," Sam said, sticking his thumbs in his belt and

leaning back in the big stuffed chair, "you are just like your father."

Then we all went into Clyde's room and just sat around and talked for a while. Mostly about school and stuff like that, and I wanted to tell Clyde that I thought I could help him if he wanted me to. I was really getting good grades in school, but I thought that Clyde might get annoyed if I mentioned it. But then Gloria said that we could study together sometime and that was cool, too.

there's people
and then
there's people

6 *Me and Clyde and Sam decided to go downtown.*
We were supposed to go down to buy me a new
mouthpiece for my sax but really we were going down
because we all had money. I had fourteen dollars,
seven that I had saved by working in the A & P in
the afternoons after school and seven that my father
gave me. He said that if I wanted a new mouthpiece
(which I did), then I would have to come up with
some money and he would match it. I came up with
seven dollars. That was actually from four days of
carrying packages for people from the A & P. Clyde
had about nine dollars and Sam had about six dollars
which was his allowance minus one dollar which he
spent on two thirty-nine-cent bags of potato chips
with garlic and a large Coke. He loved Coke.

Anyway, we were downtown and were just looking around before we went to the music store to look for a mouthpiece when all of a sudden we heard this screaming and carrying on, and we turned and saw two guys running our way. They were a little older than us and they were really running, bumping into people and everything. Then they passed us by and we heard people yelling something about stopping them. Then Sam figured it all out. They had snatched some lady's pocketbook.

"Let's get 'em," he says.

And before you know it, me and Sam and Clyde are chasing these two guys to get this lady's pocketbook back. Anyway, nobody can run too fast because it's too crowded in the shopping area. But we're gaining on these guys. I don't know why I'm running, but Sam had said, "Let's get 'em," and I was running, too. Anyway we hit a little area where there weren't too many people, and Sam caught the second guy, the guy with the pocketbook in his hand. He twisted and swung at Sam but Sam ducked and hit the guy pretty hard. The other guy had ran across the street. Then the guy that Sam hit kicked him on the knee and then turned and ran again. But he had dropped the pocketbook. Clyde and I caught up with Sam and we saw the second guy dodging cars as he ran across the street and knew that there wasn't any chance of catching him. We were about a block away from where we first saw what was happening, but we figured the lady who owned the pocketbook would come up eventually, and anyway, Sam's knee was hurt so we helped him over to the side of the building while he rolled up his pants leg and looked at his knee. Clyde had the pocketbook and Sam was looking at his knee and so was I when all of a sudden this big hand and arm goes around my neck and just about lifts me off the ground. Whoever it was that had me—I think it was the son of King Kong—slammed Clyde into the building. Another guy grabbed Sam and hit him across the face. These were grownups. Then they started talking about how they had us.

"We got them," one of them said. Well, I knew that. But what I didn't know was *why* they got us. Then this white lady runs up and starts thanking God that they didn't get away with her pocketbook when all the time she should have been thanking Fast Sam. Then two policemen came up and they grabbed us away from the first guys and put handcuffs on us. I finally realized that we were being arrested.

"Hey, man, what you putting—" Sam started saying, but the policeman just pushed him right into the wall. I could see that Sam's face was puffed up. Right over the eye. I was just about set to turn to see Clyde when I got pushed into the wall. In about another second Clyde was against the wall, too.

"This your pocketbook, ma'am?" a voice said.

"Yes, it is, officer," a woman's voice said.

Then a police car came up and they took me and Sam and Clyde to the police car and pushed us into the back seat. Sam got a bump on his head from hitting it into the top of the police car when they were pushing him into the back seat. Every time Clyde or Sam tried to say something the policeman would tell them to shut up. They put the lady in another police car and took us all away. When they got us to the police station there were a lot of people around. They took us in and put all of us in a cage after taking the handcuffs off. They left us in the cage for about ten minutes, and then they took us into a room with a lot of desks and started asking us our names and everything. We said that we didn't take the lady's pocketbook and they said things like "Yeah, sure," you know, the way people say things when they don't really believe you. Then they put us against a wall and they said it was a lineup. Sam looked awful. He really looked awful. His face was swollen in about three places but he seemed more mad than scared. Then the woman came in and a policeman asked her were we the boys that snatched her pocketbook and she said yes.

"I didn't snatch your pocketbook, lady!" Clyde yelled out, and one of the policeman went like he was going to hit Clyde and Clyde shut up. I was trembling, really. My knees were really shaking. They asked the lady if anything was missing and she looked in the pocketbook and took everything out and looked at it very carefully and then said no, that as far as she could see everything was there.

Then they made us turn around and face the wall while they felt us up on our arms and legs and sides, and then we had to empty our pockets. They asked us where we got the money that we had but they didn't believe us when we told them. One policeman, who wasn't wearing a jacket, came over and said that there had been another purse-snatching earlier. Then two other policemen came over and each one of them took one of us over to a different place and started asking us questions.

I didn't take anything and I started crying. I'm not sure why but I just started crying. The policeman said that everything was all right because I was the youngest and I wouldn't get into trouble if I just told what the others had taken. And I told him that we were just downtown to get a mouthpiece, and he asked me if I was calling the lady a liar because she had already identified us as the purse-snatchers. I said that I wasn't calling anybody a liar but we hadn't stolen anything. I tried to tell him about Sam catching the guys that had taken the pocketbook, but he just gave me a look and said that I would just have to be sent away to a home. Then me and Sam got put into a cage again. Sam and Clyde weren't crying but I sure was.

Then another guy came in and he had this red-haired woman with him and he looked at us in the cage and shook his head and started talking to the police officers, and then they brought the lady over to look at us again and she asked them to take us out of the cages, and they took us out and put us against the wall again, and then they came over and told us that we could go home. Just like that. So we all looked at each other and the lady came over and said that she was sorry, that the guys who took her pocketbook looked just like us. Actually they didn't even look near to us. And the other guy, who came in with the red-haired woman, said that he had seen the whole thing and that he was sorry that it had taken him so long to get down to the station. I was glad that he got down at all. If he had been busy or something we would have been in a world of trouble. The police asked us where we lived and they gave us carfare for the bus and told us they were sorry that they had to bring us downtown. The lady offered to give Sam five dollars but Sam told her to keep her five dollars. I don't know why he did that and it seemed stupid, but I was so glad he did it I could have jumped up and down. And that's how I got into jail again. We went on home and I told my father, and he said that I was learning what the world was all about. I don't think so, though. Because the people I like most, like Clyde and Sam and Gloria and Kitty, aren't like that. Neither are my parents but sometimes my father seems a little mean. So the second thing that got me into jail, besides modern science, was helping people. You get into jail for some very funny things.

about being unfaithful

7 *Being unfaithful to a woman can get you into a lot of trouble.* I finally decided that I was in love with Kitty Jones about a week before I was unfaithful to her. She was the prettiest girl that I had ever met and I really loved her a lot. Of course I didn't tell her that I loved her because I didn't want it to go to her head. Sam always said that you should never let a girl know that you love her or she'll start acting funny. I guess that's because Sam went up to this girl—not Kitty, who he had just had an argument with, but another girl—and told her that he loved her and she slapped him. Anyway, I was in love with Kitty until I met this girl named Susan. Susan wasn't as pretty as Kitty but she was okay. She was a friend of Gloria and kind of chubby. But one day in school we had to do some filing together in the old records room. That was part of the honor squad's duties. We were filing and talking and she asked me if I had ever kissed a girl. I said yes, plenty of times. She said that she had only kissed one boy and I asked her if she had ever soul kissed and she said no. I said that she didn't know what kissing was unless she had soul kissed. (I had never really soul kissed but at least I knew a lot about it because Sam had told me.)

"What's a soul kiss like?" Susan asked.

"That's when you put your tongue in the other person's mouth when you're kissing them," I said. "But you really have to do it before you know what it's all about."

"Would you soul kiss me?" she asked.

Now that was a problem. Because I wasn't just a kid any more. I was going on thirteen and really couldn't be fooling around with girls. You know, when you get older you have to control what you do more. But I thought I might as well give her a soul kiss so I went over to her and took her face in my hands and started to kiss her. First I just kissed her ordinary, which was really nice and I had to sort of move my body away from her, which wasn't easy because as I said she was kind of chubby, but if I hadn't she might have felt something and embarrassed me. Anyway, then I was just about to soul kiss her when she started to soul kiss me! I had never felt so funny in my entire life. It was a long kiss, too. And she held me very close, too. I knew that Susan was older than me, nearly fourteen I think, but I didn't really care. After we had finished kissing she just looked at me for a while, and then she asked me if I would soul kiss her, and I said yes and I kissed her, only my tongue wasn't nearly as long as hers was and I don't think it was as good but she seemed to enjoy it. That's just about when I fell in love with her. She started asking me things like where I lived and did I have a girl friend. I knew I had been in love with Kitty but I had never kissed Kitty or anything. I had kissed Susan.

After we had kissed a third time she asked me if I played basketball on the school team and if I knew any karate. Well, I had to tell her that I didn't play ball on the school team but I told her that I did know a little karate. I had seen a trick on television and I thought that I'd try it with Susan. On television one guy would be blindfolded and the other guy would stand there with a handkerchief in his hand. The guy with the handkerchief in his hand would throw it in the air and just as it came down he would holler "NOW!" and the other guy would snatch off his blindfold and then jump up and kick the handkerchief before it fell. I told Susan about this and she blindfolded me and threw up a piece of Kleenex, which was because she didn't have two handkerchiefs. When she yelled, "NOW!" I snatched off the handkerchief, jumped up and dealt a death kick to the corner of the filing cabinet. The pain was something awful. I fell on the floor and rolled over. I grabbed my foot but it was hurt too much to touch. Susan went out to get the school nurse.

The school nurse came down about two minutes later and asked me what happened. I told her that I hurt my foot.

"How?" she said.

What difference did it make *how?* What was I going to say? I mean, really, what was I going to say? "Well, I was soul kissing Susan, and I had seen this trick on television, see, and I thought that if Susan saw me do it . . ."

The school nurse felt my foot after I got my shoe off and I jumped around and hollered a lot because the pain was, as I said before, something else! She said that I had to go to the hospital right away. The custodian drove me to the hospital in his car. They took me to the emergency ward and I got an X-ray and everything. The doctor said that I had what they called a hairline fracture. Which means it was broken a little. Oh, yes, I forgot to say that BB went to the hospital with me. She was on the safety patrol in school and the nurse had her come to the hospital with me. I wasn't the least bit nervous or anything like that, even though it hurt a lot, but it was still good having BB come with me to the hospital. And at least I had a broken foot, too. Anything that I can't stand is somebody going to the hospital and they can't find anything wrong. But I had a definite hairline fracture, the doctor said. He asked me how I got the break and I told him. He told me that he gets more karate fractures than any other kind, especially since Kung Fu moved to prime time on the television. Anyway, when we finished fixing my foot up, which was mostly the doctor taping it up and giving me this big white sock to wear over the tape, I was told that I could go home. The doctor asked me if I had another friend besides BB that could help me home. And BB said that she would call Clyde. She went to make the call and a moment or two later came back and said that she couldn't reach Clyde but that Sam was coming over to give me a hand.

The school nurse, who was still there, said that she thought that I'd be all right and she would see me in a week. This was because the doctor told me to stay off the foot for about a week. They even gave me some crutches to use. You should have seen how concerned BB was. Anyway, I had to stay off the foot for a week and then come back again for X-rays. The school nurse signed some papers and we all left. Sam had got there and me, him, and BB went home by cab.

good-bye forever: at least

8 *When we got to my house we found Maria sitting on the stoop crying. We asked her what the matter was and she said that Kitty had disappeared, and no one knew where she was.*

"Angel and Clyde and Cap are out looking for her now. Here's the note she left."

I looked at the note.

CLYDE

I am going away and I will never be back. I can't stand to live here any more. I might come back when I am grown and married.

Good-bye forever,
Ms KITTY JONES

"That's just it. Nobody knows why she ran away or anything. Her mother's not even home and she doesn't know about it."

"Did Clyde call the police?"

"He didn't want to call the police because then everything would be upset. We checked the handwriting on the note and it looks like hers so we don't think she was kidnaped. Anyway, Clyde don't think she was kidnaped. They're going around to all her friends' places. You know Jeannie, that new girl? You know her BB."

BB nodded that she did.

"Well, she's upstairs in case the phone rings and I'm sitting down here in case she comes around."

"Maybe she's just fooling around," Sam said.

"I don't think so because she don't be fooling around like that." Maria wiped at her eyes.

"Did they check over at that girl's house where she does her homework sometimes?"

"Everywhere. They even checked on 118th Street, and you know that Kitty would never go there by herself," Maria said. "It's almost eight thirty and she's usually home about at least seven. At least if it was real winter she might get cold and come home, but it's warm."

You could see that Maria was real sad. I didn't know what to do. Sam and BB mentioned some more places to look, but Maria said that they had looked in every place Sam and BB mentioned. Then Clyde and Cap came back and said they still couldn't find Kitty. We just stood around for a while mentioning places where she might have gone but anywhere we mentioned had already been checked out. Angel came by a little later and he said that he hadn't had any luck either but he had asked his mother to let him and Maria stay out later and help look for Kitty, and their mother said okay.

It was almost nine o'clock so I had to go home. I asked them to call me if they heard anything and they said they would. Clyde was real quiet, not just worried, and I wondered about that.

When I got home I told my mother what had happened to Kitty and she said that Kitty had probably just went off to a movie or something and had forgotten to tell Clyde that she was going. She fixed me a hamburger and I had that and some milk for dinner.

I had to tell my father all over about how I had hurt my foot. He went through this big thing as if he didn't believe it could really happen the way I said it did.

"Why on earth did you bang your foot into a file cabinet? That doesn't make a bit of sense. Not one bit."

It was no use telling him that I didn't mean to hit the cabinet, because once he got wound up you might as well forget it. He was going on with the same thing until he had talked himself out. That's the way he was. I got out my sax to practice, and he immediately jumped on me again. This time about how if I spent more time on school work and less on the sax maybe I wouldn't be breaking my foot against file cabinets.

Mama said that I could go up to the roof and practice if I wanted to. She had a way of saying that you *could* do something when she really meant that you *had* to do it. I could see that she didn't want me to get into it with my father and was just being cool and all. So I took my sax, crutches and all, to the roof. Our roof was fenced in all around and sometimes women came up with their children if they didn't feel like taking them to the park. They didn't allow dogs up on the roof, either.

I put my sax together and started to get into one of my cool attitudes. I had about three real cool attitudes that I got into. One was on the way home from a spy movie. That's when I pretended I was in England or Poland or any of those places where they have cobblestone streets. Then I did my cool spy thing.

Another cool attitude was when I pretended that I was Clyde. Because—well, Clyde's cool. I mean, he walked cool and he acted cool and even when he didn't seem so cool, when you thought about it later, he was cool.

The last cool attitude, and, maybe, the coolest, was when I play my sax on the roof. That's *really* cool. I saw this picture on television once where this guy would go up on his roof and play this song on his guitar. Then he met this girl and they were in love for a while but then they broke up over something. Then one day he was drinking some whiskey and was on the roof thinking about jumping off, and all the while he was playing his guitar, real cool, and she came up and walked real close to him and started humming the same tune and they stared at each other a long time, being in love and whatnot, until the commercial came on.

I had played about two or three notes—the reed wasn't even real wet yet—when I heard somebody call my name. I must have jumped near a foot. I was scared almost to death. Like I said, I'm kind of scary anyway. I had goose pimples all over. Then I heard the voice again, coming from the darkness, only this time I knew it was Kitty.

"Kitty?"

"Yes."

I went over to her on my crutches. She was sitting on an old milk box that someone had fastened a cushion to so they could use it as a chair. She had Clyde's school jacket around her shoulders.

"Everybody's looking for you," I said. "Clyde was even searching around 118th Street."

"Could you call him for me?"

"Clyde?"

"Yes."

There wasn't much light on the roof. But from the light there was, which came from a bulb over the roof door, and the moon which was just shining through the clouds, I could see most of Kitty's face. She looked older. She still looked like a little girl, but like an old little girl. I went to the side of the roof where there was a narrow alleyway between the two buildings and called down for Clyde. I knew if he was home he'd hear me but if he wasn't I'd have to go all the way downstairs. I called twice and finally BB answered. I told her to tell Clyde to come up. She said okay and I figured that she would guess that Kitty was on the roof, too.

Clyde came up and BB, Gloria, and Sam. Angel and Maria and Cap had went on home.

"C'mon, let's go home." Clyde put his arm around his sister. I knew then that something had went wrong and that Clyde knew what it was. Otherwise he would have asked Kitty what the matter was. But Sam asked, anyway.

"What's the matter, Kitty?"

She didn't really answer Sam but said that she didn't want to go home again, ever. Clyde had his head down and they looked as if they had the same feeling.

"What's going on, Clyde?" Gloria asked him. Clyde took a deep breath, started to say something, and then stopped.

He looked down for a while and then Sam sat next to him.

"Why don't you play something, Stuff?" Sam said.

At first I didn't even understand him because I wasn't expecting him to say that but then I did understand him. I looked at Gloria and she looked at me.

"Go ahead, Stuff," she said, "play something."

I couldn't figure out why they wanted me to play something just then. Anyway I put the practice mute in the sax so it wouldn't sound too loud and I started in playing the song everybody at school said that I played the best. It was a song that I liked called "Mood Indigo," and it seemed to fill in the spaces caused by everyone not talking. I wondered if my mother could hear me playing. She loved to hear me play and I loved playing for her. I realized that I loved playing for my friends even more. It was the first time, really, that my friends meant more to me than my mother, and I thought that I would have to figure it all out later if I could. But right then I had to concentrate on the playing.

For some reason the music seemed to be more a part of me than it had ever been before. It was like pushing myself into the horn, what I felt and all, and having it come out still being me but being music at the same time.

I played the whole song, and then the roof was quiet again except for the noises that came from the apartments below. And they all blended together to make one noise that must be the unofficial city noise. I was wondering if I should play something else when Clyde started talking.

"Did you see my mother tonight?" he asked, to no one in particular. Gloria said no, that she hadn't.

"Well, she went out with this guy she met on her job." Clyde shrugged.

"What for?" Sam asked.

"'Cause she wanted to, that's why!" Kitty was sniffling.

"Kitty feels bad because Mama went out with this guy. I don't really want to talk about it." Clyde was feeling bad, too. I didn't know what was going on, but BB and Gloria seemed to know about it.

"It ain't no big thing, Clyde," Gloria said. "I know you might not dig it, but she's not doing anything wrong. Is she?"

"Why she have to go out with him in the first place?" Kitty said.

"Is he mean or something?" I asked.

"Why don't you go on home, Stuff," Gloria said.

At first I didn't answer but then Gloria said it again, about why didn't I go on home. I didn't want to go home, that's why.

"Clyde, do I have to leave?" I asked.

"No, man," he answered. "You know what's happening, Stuff, is that my mom went on a date with this guy, see, and I just find it hard to take. And Kitty finds it hard to take, too. Right, baby?"

"I thought she loved Daddy." Kitty half talked and half cried. "I don't want this guy for a father."

"He can't be our father," Clyde said. "He'll have to be a stepfather. Or maybe a foster father."

"How can Mommy *do* something like that? I mean, how *can* she?"

"Hey, Clyde, Kitty"—Sam knelt down in front of them—"it ain't the world, man. You know, the guy could be okay, or maybe she won't even go out with him again."

"Hey, Sam, why don't you shut up your mouth, man." Clyde stood up and pushed Sam. That was the first time I had ever seen Clyde really mad at Sam.

"You don't have to be pushing on me, Clyde," Sam came back. "I don't have to take that, you know. Even from you."

"Well, why don't you do something about it." Clyde pushed Sam again. "You don't know nothing about what's going on so why don't you shut up!"

"It ain't the world, Clyde." Gloria stepped in between Sam and Clyde. "I know what's going on even if you think Sam doesn't. My mother's all alone and I've been thinking about what's going to happen with us. And I've been thinking about it longer than you have. And even if Sam don't feel the same thing you do, you don't have any right hitting on him."

"I have all the right I want to have!" Clyde said.

"Why?" BB asked. "Because you're hurt now because things aren't going too tough for you, right? But how about me? I wanted to join the club because things weren't too tough for me, either. And now as soon as things look a little bad for you, all the things that were part of the club are just gone, right?"

Clyde looked around at all of us and then he looked

at Kitty and sat back down and put his arm around her again.

"You see, I loved my father very much," Kitty said, "and I feel very bad about my mother going out with some other guy. I don't want another father and she don't care about my father's being dead and all, like me and Clyde do. That's the whole problem. All she wants is to go out and have a good time and all. How do you think I feel—my father's spirit could be walking around the house and trying to be at home and here she comes up to the house with another guy. If she loves my father, why she have to go out with that guy for?"

Nobody had anything to say. We just stood around for a while, and then Sam asked me if I thought the Los Angeles Lakers were going to win the Western Division title this year. I didn't know. I hardly even knew who was on their team this year. We stood around for some more time, talking about this and that, when the door to the roof opened and it was Clyde's mother.

"What are you people up to?" she said. Her voice always had a little laugh in it. A man came up with her.

"Nothing," Kitty said.

"Is something wrong?" Mrs. Jones put her hand on Kitty's shoulder and Kitty pushed it off.

"Let's go downstairs," Clyde said.

"How come you had to go out with him?" Kitty asked.

Everyone turned toward the man that was standing with Mrs. Jones. He was tall and wore glasses and looked a little bit like my father except that he was smoking and my father never smoked.

"I don't think that I have to answer to my children about what I do," Mrs. Jones said. Her voice was low but still kind of shaky.

"And I don't have to go and live with you any more, either!" Kitty began to cry again. As soon as she started Mrs. Jones started and Clyde put his arm around Kitty and they started downstairs. The guy that Mrs. Jones had went out with started to say something but she just walked away from him. So Clyde and Kitty and Mrs. Jones left, and me, Sam, BB, and Gloria were left on the roof with the guy.

"Can I say something?" he asked.

"Go ahead, talk is free," said BB.

"Well, let me tell you something." The guy leaned against the brick wall that separated our roof from the next. He was smoking a pipe and he took out a match and relit it. When I saw his face in the light from the match he didn't look so bad. "Sometimes we get very close to another person. Oh, that person may be a friend, or a brother or a sister or even a husband or a wife. And if something happens, if that person that we're real close to happens to die, then we've lost somebody, a friend who we love very much or a relative who we love very much but it doesn't mean that we should die, too. Mrs. Jones's children loved their father very much, I'm sure, but that doesn't mean that they're not going to grow up and get married. That doesn't mean that they're going to stop living. Mr. Jones wouldn't want to see his children unhappy after he's gone. He wouldn't want to see his wife unhappy, either. And sometimes it's hard, you know, if you've lost someone that you really care for, that's lived with you and shared your life with you, it's hard to lose them. After they're gone you feel bad because you've lost them, but after a while you feel bad because you're all alone. And after a while you wonder which is worse, losing someone or being alone."

"I'm alone." My voice even scared me. But it was true. I loved my mother and Sharon and all, even my father, I guess, because he's really not so bad as I always put on, but I wasn't in love with anybody. Not the way they meant *in love* when they did it in the movies.

"Well, that's because you're young. And when you're very young you have a lot of casual friends and you're more interested in playing ball and running around having fun than anything else. When you get older you don't have as many friends. The friends you do have are different. When you're married you stick with your husband or with your wife. Like your parents do. But when one of them goes away or dies, then you're all alone again. You're all alone so you go to a movie with a friend. Is that really so bad?"

I didn't think it was so bad but I decided not to

say anything. I kind of knew that everyone there knew a little bit more than I did.

"Later, I got to split." Sam said that he had to leave and he sort of be-bopped away. Then Gloria and BB left and just me and the guy were there. It kind of bothered me because I didn't know if the others were mad at him or not, and I didn't want to be the only one that was friends with him if everyone else was mad. So I gathered up my stuff and I told him that I had to leave.

The next day I saw Clyde and he asked me what the guy had said. The guy's name was William, by the way. I kind of told him what little I knew. Clyde said that his mother had run a lot of things down to him and he understood them some.

"I got it with my head," he said. "And that's funny because in school I keep trying to get things with my head. I've got this with my head but I don't really feel it. My moms ran it all down about how she was lonely and about how she wouldn't do anything to put down my father and all, but I don't feel it. Kitty's still upset. So is Gloria."

I asked him how come Gloria was upset. The guy wasn't going out with *her* mother. But Clyde said that she thought her mother might go out with somebody because her father had split. And just knowing that it was a possibility made her feel closer to it than I did. I didn't really understand that, either.

But I didn't mind. I had found out that there was

a lot of things that I didn't understand. And even though it was better if I knew what was going on all the time and understood everything, I found out that if I didn't know everything it was okay, too. I really felt close to Kitty, and I asked her, after a while, how she felt about it. I told her that I liked her, too. I wanted to tell her that I liked her a whole lot but I got ashamed. She told me that she was real mad at her mother for going out with that guy even though she didn't feel that her mother was doing wrong or anything like that. I asked her why and she didn't know. I kind of think it was because she felt her father might not be her father any more if her mother was going out with somebody else. Everybody seemed to feel one way but couldn't go along with the way they felt because it didn't seem right. Nobody felt that Clyde's mother should go out with another man, but they knew it was really okay.

Anyway, I was falling in love with Kitty all over again. She told me that she liked me a lot, too. I was going to ask her to be my girl friend, but I was afraid she might say no and tell everybody so I didn't ask her.

Mrs. Jones didn't go on another date for a long time. It was over a year later. But when she did, it was Kitty that got upset again. Clyde took it real cool. He didn't even mind when she went out with another guy, but Kitty went into a panic kind of thing. By the time Mrs. Jones had went out with another guy me and Kitty were real close. Everybody knew that we were going out together and everything, but even I couldn't help her. She just got so upset. I really wished I understood, but I didn't.

chalky

9 *You ever see one of those old-time movies when a guy looks at something, then looks away, and then looks back at it real quick? They call that a double take. Well, I saw Sam do a triple take or at least a two-and-a-half take. There was this new guy that used to hang around the center a lot and talk about how bad he was. He used to say things like he was the best basketball player that we had ever seen and that he had had a tryout with the Chicago Bulls but then they found out that he was only fifteen and a half years old. We didn't believe him but every time we had a game he said that he didn't want to play because we really weren't enough competition. Sam challenged him to a one-on-one game and he said okay and everybody thought we were really going to find* out how good he was, but just as he was lacing up his sneakers he looks over at Sam and says, "Hey, man, what we playing for? I usually play for five a point."

"What you mean, 'five a point'?" Sam asked.

"You know, if you beat me by four points I owe you twenty dollars. And if I beat you by four points you owe me twenty dollars."

"I don't have any twenty dollars," Sam said.

"I thought you wanted to play some ball, turkey," Chalky said and took his sneakers off.

Sam sat back down again. Now, later, me and Clyde were talking with Angel and we figured that Chalky knew Sam didn't have that kind of money to be betting five dollars a point. And we also said that we knew Sam was a good basketball player and if they had been betting a nickel a point Sam would have bet him and played. But five dollars a point was a lot of money! Angel said that maybe he really did almost make the Chicago Bulls. We still didn't really believe it, but if a guy had the heart to bet five dollars a point he had to be pretty good. And he was just about a little taller than Sam, too. That night after dinner when I should have been doing my homework I daydreamed about Chalky and Sam in a one-on-one basketball match. At least it started with Chalky and Sam, but it ended with Chalky and me. I won, too. I have never, ever lost an imaginary basketball game. When I'm depressed I sometimes miss imaginary shots, though.

One day Clyde said that we should all go up to his house. So we did and we put some records on and sat around and talked about basketball and stuff. All of us were there, Clyde (naturally—it was his house), Sam, me, Chalky, Angel, and Light Billy. Light Billy had actually moved by this time but still used to come around the block sometimes. Then someone started talking about girls. Lately a lot of the guys were talking about girls a lot. This particular conversation got started when Light Billy asked Clyde how his sister Kitty was doing. Clyde said okay and that she was downtown taking piano lessons. Then Chalky said that he was talking to a girl named Gloria yesterday, and he asked if anybody knew her. We said yes, we all knew Gloria, which was the truth. Then Chalky asked if any of us were going with her and everybody said no. The truth of the matter is, though, that Sam had taken her to the movies a couple of times. But they weren't officially girl friend or boy friend, I guess. Although I don't know what makes it official, anyway. Then Chalky did it. He asked Clyde if he could use his telephone. Clyde didn't know at first because none of us ever asked Clyde if we could use his phone. That was because we never had a reason to call anybody hardly. Anyway, Clyde said he guessed he could as long as it wasn't long distance. Then Chalky takes out this little piece of paper he had in his wallet and dials a number.

"It's this chick I spoke to yesterday," he said. "I

got her telephone number." He winked at us. Sam
looked at me, and I looked at Clyde, and Light Billy
kind of raised his eyebrows. Chalky put his finger to
his lips to tell us to keep quiet and then he winked
again. "Hello, Gloria? This is Chalky. Remember you
spoke to me yesterday. . . . Right. Look, I happen to
be in the neighborhood and I wondered if I could
come up and talk to you about something for a few
minutes. . . . Well, I'll tell you when I get there. . . .
Yeah. In about ten minutes. . . . Okay. Later, sweet-
heart."

Then he hung up. Everybody wanted to know what
he wanted to talk to Gloria about but nobody wanted
to ask. But Chalky told us anyway.

"I'm going to go up there and see if I can get
some," he said, and then he went through his wallet
until he found a little red and white thing. He held
it up so we could see it, put it back in his wallet, and
left.

Now, when he held it up was when Sam did this
triple take. Then he looked at me and Clyde and then
he looked away. Afterwards, after Chalky had left, we
just sat around talking about basketball again but Sam
didn't say much. After a while everybody left except
me and Sam and Clyde and we were hardly saying
anything. I knew what was on everybody's mind,
though. It was Chalky going up to Gloria's house.
Well, it was more than that. He was talking about
"getting some" from Gloria, and I knew he meant sex.

"Do you think that Gloria's going to . . . you know?" I asked.

"With who? With who? You mean that guy Chalky? You got to be kidding. What are you—stupid or something?" Sam was really upset. You could tell because his voice was so high. Whenever he got excited his voice would get real high. "In the first place Gloria ain't that kind of girl."

"You want to give her a call?" Clyde asked.

"No. I don't care what she do," Sam responded.

"You want to play some three-handed hearts?"

"No."

We just sat around for a while, watched some television, and then we split up and went home. The next day was Sunday and right after church Sam went over to Gloria's house. She wasn't home yet because she was Catholic and went to a late Mass. So he hung around in front of the house and waited until she did come home. When she came home he talked to her for a little while and then she had to leave to go someplace with her mother. Clyde and I were standing on the stoop as usual, and when Sam joined us I figured he was going to tell me and Clyde what had happened between Chalky and Gloria. But then my father came down and told me that I had to take Sharon and her girl friend over to the Apollo and find out what time the show was over so I could pick them up later. I was going to give him a little lip, but then I found that Sharon was going to the show with Kitty,

Clyde's sister. I didn't even know they were friends. Anyway, so I didn't get to find out what happened on Sunday because when I came back I couldn't find either Clyde or Sam, which really ticked me off because after all I was taking Clyde's sister to the show, too. I went up to Clyde's house and nobody was home, and I went up to Sam's house and his mother told me she hadn't seen him since early morning. I wondered if they could be at Gloria's house but I decided not to go there.

When we got home the next day from school it was really cold. I mean really cold. And there were some new people moving into the building next to mine so we all had to stand around and see what they had. You know you can tell a lot about somebody if you watch them move in. Anyway, they had two kids. One was about my age and the other was about four or five years older. In fact I don't even know if you would call her a kid. But then we went up to my place, which was about the first time we ever had gone there. Usually we went up to Sam's place or Clyde's or Gloria's and sometimes even Cap's or Angel's. Angel's place was especially cool because his mother always fed you. You would say you weren't hungry but it didn't mean anything to her. You went to her house and you ate.

So we go to my house and guess what Sharon does? She goes out with her own money and buys some sodas and some cookies. Can you imagine that? She's

only ten. And then she knocks on my door and I give
out this little look and say come in and she comes
in with the cookies on a plate and says that there are
more cookies and sodas in the kitchen and that she
was going to the library. I really felt good about that.

Anyway, we talk around a little bit and then I asked
Clyde and Sam where they were yesterday. They said
that they had went over to the park and shot around.
Then they started talking about whether Sam should
go out for the school basketball team or whether he
should switch this year to an academic course. I
waited a little while and then asked, trying to act
casual, about what happened with Chalky and Gloria.

"What do you think happened? Nothing!" Sam
looked at Clyde and I could see that Clyde didn't
know anything more than I did. "Chalky went up to
talk his stuff and Gloria told him to cop a walk. I
told her what he had said when we were over at
Clyde's house."

"You told her?" Clyde asked.

"Yeah."

"Everything?"

"Yeah."

"What did you say?"

"I said that he said he was going to come over to
see if he could get some." Fast Sam was eating twice
as many cookies as me and Clyde put together. "She
said, 'Get some what?' and I said, 'Some you-know,'
and she said that she didn't know, and I said some

sex. Then she got mad and wanted to go over to Chalky's house and tell him off. She really got mad. She said he came over and she was helping her mother snap some beans, you know, getting dinner ready, and he says could he see her alone. So she takes him on into the living room and asks him what he wanted, and he started talking about let's sit on the couch and she told him that she had to help her mother. You know, she and her moms is real close now.

"Anyway, he keeps talking about let's sit on the couch because he wanted to tell her something important. So she finally sits down on the couch and he starts telling her about how fine she looks and tries to put his arm around her. Then she just told him to split 'cause she was busy, and he left and said he'd give her a call."

"I knew that cat was jive," Clyde said.

"He's a chump, that's what he is!" Sam continued.

"Did you tell her about that thing he had?" I asked.

"Yeah, I told her. She really got mad after that. We talked for longer than we ever talked before. I asked her something, what she thought about Chalky wanting to try something like that. She said she would never do anything like that, especially with a guy she didn't love. So I asked her if she would with somebody she loved, you know."

"What did she say?"

"She said that she didn't know. That gave me some ideas. I mean, Gloria and me are pretty tight." Sam took a sip from my soda. "I didn't say anything to her then, but I was thinking that maybe I would ask her for some myself."

"You ever do it to a girl before?" I asked.

"Sure, man," Sam said, finishing my soda.

"Who?" asked Clyde.

"I don't want to say because it's a secret."

"It's a secret because it's not true," Clyde said, "because as big as your mouth is if you had done it you'd have it in the newspaper on the front page."

"Man, I got secrets you don't even know about," Sam said.

"Like what?"

"Did you know it was me that broke Mrs. Lucas's window last summer?"

"You broke that window?"

"Right. I found that baseball and was imaginary pitching and the ball got loose. I was going to go over and say that I did it and everything, but when she started yelling about how she was going to call the cops I sneaked away. You know who saw me?"

"Who?"

"Angel's sister."

"But you still didn't do it to a girl," Clyde said.

"Well, I almost did once. I went up to this girl's house and we fooled around a lot. I don't want to tell you how far I got," Sam said. "You ever do it to a girl?"

"Nope."

"You?"

Sam was looking at me and I couldn't help but grin. No, I never "did it" to a girl and they knew it.

"What you think, Clyde? You think I should ask Gloria for some?" Sam looked over at Clyde while he scraped the crumbs up with his fingertips. "She said that she might do it if she liked somebody enough. And I think she likes me. I might give her a little play. What do you think?"

"Hey, look. Weren't you mad with Chalky because Chalky said the same thing?" Clyde said. I hoped that he wouldn't end the conversation, because I liked talking about sex. It was really something that I wanted to know about.

"Do you put me in the same class as Chalky?" Sam asked.

"That wasn't the question. You got mad when Chalky said he wanted to get some from Gloria and now you're saying the same thing, right?"

"You figure that nobody should do it before they're married," Sam said, "but I know a lot of people do."

"I'm not saying you shouldn't. I don't even know, but I do know that you were mad when Chalky said it, and I don't see the difference."

"The difference is that I like Gloria a lot and he just wants to get some."

"You doing her a favor?"

"No, but she could do me a favor if she gave me some. You know I like her." Sam was looking uncomfortable.

"All I wondered is what makes you different from

Chalky?" Clyde asked. "I mean you know you and I are tight and everything, but, like, from Gloria's point of view. What's the difference? What are you giving her?" Clyde went on. "Say that making out with a girl is a dynamite feeling, okay? Well, remember that girl that got pregnant last year in school? She got that baby for life. And even if the baby didn't make it, everybody knew that she was pregnant. Or remember that girl those guys from Lenox said they were going to go mess with?"

"I didn't go over there and I didn't see her," Sam said. "You see, you're making a big thing of this and all I did was ask a question. It ain't no big thing."

"But that's how people get babies," I said. "And that's a big thing."

"Okay, so I won't ask Gloria," Sam said.

"We ought to get her up here and ask her," Clyde said.

"You mean all of us ask her for some?" I asked.

"No, turkey! I mean just to get her opinion on the subject."

"You can't talk to girls about sex," Sam said. "You know how they are. She'll probably start giggling or something."

"If you don't talk to girls about sex how are you going to ask her for some?" Clyde asked.

"How come you have to twist everything around? Huh?" Sam was getting mad and his voice was getting higher. "You know what I meant. Let's just drop the whole subject, man."

We sat around awhile. I wet my finger and picked up some of the cookie crumbs with it. Then I remembered that Sharon said there was some more cookies and stuff in the kitchen and I went and got it. When I came back Sam and Clyde were still sitting around not talking. I put the cookies down and right away you could see that Sam was interested in them. The first cookies we had were vanilla wafers, and these were chocolate cookies with cream. Who ever invented chocolate cookies with cream must have been some kind of a genius.

"What about the club?" Clyde asked. "We said we'd talk about our problems, right?"

"Well, it ain't no problem now because I'm not going to ask her for none. In fact, if she walked in here right now—if the Queen of England walked in here right now and said, 'Please, Sam, take some, honey,' I still wouldn't do it."

"Look, Sam, I'm not on your case, man. But it's a problem and you know that. How many sisters you see getting pregnant? A lot, right?" Clyde looked at Sam.

"I didn't get nobody pregnant. What you running your mouth on me for?" Sam scooped nearly half the plate of cookies up and looked away from Clyde. I had never noticed how big his hands were before. No wonder he could handle a basketball.

"I told you I'm off your case. But it's still a problem, right? Dig, would you marry a girl with a baby?"

"I don't know." Sam's voice was muffled because he had his mouth full of cookies.

"But you sure would think about it, wouldn't you?" Clyde asked.

Sam shrugged.

"Would you marry a girl with a baby?" Clyde was talking to me.

"Yeah!" I said. I liked the idea of getting married. And I liked babies, too.

"You're a snap, Stuff," Sam said. Then he put out his hand and Clyde gave him five. "Okay, look, call Gloria up and we'll ask her opinion but don't tell her that I was going to ask her for some. Okay?"

"Okay." So Clyde called Gloria and sure enough she was home. He asked her if she'd come over to his place, that we wanted to discuss something with her. She must have asked him what because he started grinning and then had to try twice before he told her. She asked him who all was over to his house, and he said me and Sam were over. Then he hung up and said Gloria said that she would be over in about fifteen minutes.

Then Clyde said that we had to be cool when Gloria came over. You know, we couldn't crack up or anything.

"Excuse me, Miss Gloria." Sam was talking in a deep voice and holding a pencil in front of Clyde like it was a microphone. "What do you think about sex?"

Then we all cracked up. Then Sam got real serious and Clyde got real serious and we were quiet for about a minute. Then Clyde looked over at Sam like he was going to laugh any minute, and Sam looked over at me, and I wouldn't have laughed except I had a cookie in my mouth so I cracked up, and then Clyde and Sam cracked up again, and then we couldn't stop cracking up. Clyde was trying to be a little cool but then he'd look at Sam or look at me and we'd all start laughing again. And Sam had this real high laugh that sounded a little bit like a squeaky door that somebody was messing with. Anyway, this went on for a while with Sam asking some funny questions every so often in his radio-announcer voice until the doorbell rang. Clyde gave us a look and then went to the door. Sam and me were looking at each other, making faces and about to crack again, when they came in.

Gloria had got Angel's sister, Maria, and BB and they all came in together. And they were looking ready! They all sat down and were looking so serious that Sam had a hard time swallowing his cookies.

"So what y'all want to talk about?" Gloria had her head leaning over to one side.

Sam looked at Clyde and Clyde looked at Sam and then they both looked at me. I looked down real quick because I wasn't going to start a conversation about sex with one girl, let alone three. Finally Clyde spoke.

"We were talking about, you know, and since you were in the club we figured we'd ask your opinion." Clyde wasn't looking at Gloria when he spoke.

"Well, I figured"—Gloria was looking dead at

Clyde—"that since you had three guys up here I'd bring some girls to even things out. And I thought the conversation was going to be about sex, not 'you know.'"

"Right!" Sam spoke up. I guess he figured he'd already talked to Gloria about sex so he could do it again. "We were talking about whether or not guys should try to get some."

"Some what?" Gloria asked.

"You know," Sam answered.

"What's all this 'you know' stuff? What are you talking about?" That was BB.

"Why don't you?" Maria asked. She had a little bit of a Spanish accent.

"Why don't we?" Clyde looked up at her.

"Why don't you get some from Sam, Clyde?" When Maria said "Clyde" she said it so it rhymed with "reed."

"Now what's that supposed to mean?" Clyde asked. He looked like he was going to get mad, and I got on one of my tough looks. It would have been tougher if I had my hat on.

"What it means, Clyde Jones," Gloria said, "is that 'getting some' is done with a guy and a girl. So what we should be talking about is whether a guy and a girl should get together and do something. Not if a guy should do it. So when we talk about it, let's talk about it as a together thing. Because, according to Hygiene 103, at least the way Miss Perlman teaches it, it's done in two's."

"Okay, then the question is should guys and girls do it?" Clyde said. He started fooling around with his sneaker.

"I don't think people should have sex before they're married," Maria said. "It's easy going around having sex but it don't prove nothing. Then if you get a baby or something, everybody looking at you like you're dirt. Even girls who've had more sex than you look at you like you're dirt. I had a cousin who got pregnant from just one time and nobody came to her side except her mother, me, and my godfather. That's all."

"Yeah, but you talk about it as if something's always going to happen," Sam said. "A lot of people do it and don't get pregnant."

"I'm hip," said Gloria. "Half the people who have sex don't get pregnant. The boys."

"Gloria, you've got an attitude," Clyde said, "that's why you can't discuss it."

"She's supposed to have an attitude," BB said. "If a girl gets pregnant by some guy she's the one who has to have it and maybe get on welfare. And then if the boy marries her he acts like he doing her a favor. She might not even want to get married to him."

"Then why she have sex with him if she don't want to marry him?" Sam asked. I thought that was a pretty good question.

"Because he might come on with—" BB started but Gloria interrupted.

"What are you guys talking about? Married sex or unmarried sex? If you're talking about getting married to somebody, that's a whole nother conversation. Because what married people do is their business. Because it's legal and ain't nobody going to say nothing about it. What you guys are talking about is sex when you're not married. Now that we got that straight you can go on, BB."

"Right," BB said. "You talking about getting some but you're not talking about what you're going to do if somebody gets pregnant or if they catch V. D."

"Okay, now we got your opinion," Clyde said. "You don't think that people should do it before they're married."

"That's what I think," said Maria.

"I think Maria's right," said BB.

"I really don't know." Gloria took the very last cookie just when I started to reach for it. She gave me a little smile. "Maybe it's right and maybe it's wrong but the way I feel, it's too important to be just doing without thinking about. You got a reason to do it, Sam?"

"Well, you know, I'm a man and it's natural that I'd want to. You know?"

"No, Sam, I don't know. Because if it's natural for you to do it because you're a man and it's not natural for me then who are you going to do it with? It's natural for me, too, but not just to take lightly. I guess if I really dug somebody I'd think about it. But I'd think about it real hard. And I hope that if a guy wants me to be with him in sex he'll find me important enough to think about it real hard. That's just the way I feel."

"I figure that if a guy can't make it with me because I don't go to bed with him, then he loves that more than he loves me, anyway," Maria said.

"A lot of people talk about it and want to do it for so many reasons that seem wrong. It don't prove nothing to me. It doesn't make me more grown, more mature, more hip, nothing," BB said. "What do you think, Clyde?"

"I think about it. But I guess it's nothing I have to do. I guess I will think about it before I do it, though." Clyde leaned back in his chair and put his hands behind his head. "I wouldn't want to get a girl pregnant if I didn't want to marry her. I wouldn't want to catch a disease either."

"That V.D. can mess with you, too," Sam said. "I guess you're right."

"What do you think, Stuff?" BB asked.

All of a sudden my face started to burn and I looked down. I was so embarrassed. I didn't know what I thought. I couldn't say anything, really. I just kind of shrugged after a while.

Later when I got home my father asked me where I was and I told him I was over to Clyde's house talking about sex. Just like that. My mother stopped rinsing out a pan and turned toward me and so did Sharon.

"With some girls, too." And I went into my room.

That wasn't the last time we talked about sex, either. For the whole next year there was a lot of talk about it, and sometimes I thought that Sam and Clyde had changed their minds, and then sometimes I wasn't sure. I don't think they were doing any sex but they were sure talking a lot about it.

chalky II

10 So what happens is that we're all sitting around the center waiting for the basketball tryouts for the center team. All of our group was there and a few guys from around the center. I counted everyone there. Mr. Reese had said that only the guys who showed up the first day with written permission from their parents could make the team. There were seventeen guys there, and Mr. Reese had told us that there were going to be fourteen guys on the team. That meant that only three guys weren't going to make it. Well, one guy I knew I had beat. And I thought I could beat a couple of other guys there, too, so I wasn't too worried. Chalky was there too.

Chalky walks in and he's got this little bag with his stuff in it. He goes into the locker room and comes out with this uniform on that said Chicago Flyers. The uniform is brand-new-looking and Sam looks at Clyde and at me and we all kind of smile. Then the ball bounces near Chalky and he picks it up and throws the ball toward the basket. He misses by about a yard and Sam cracks up.

"Hey, man, I thought you could play some ball," Sam says.

"You want to play some one on one?" Chalky asks.

"What you playing for this time," Sam asks, "a hundred dollars a point?"

"We can play for fun if you want to," Chalky says. "I got to warm up so I can make the team, anyway."

"Take the ball out, turkey," Sam says.

Clyde cleared the court and everyone stood around while Chalky and Sam started to play against each other.

First Chalky took the ball out and started dribbling toward the key, and Sam just drifted back and let him come. Then Chalky tried a little jump shot that rolled around the basket and fell in. Then Sam took the ball out and dribbled fast down the right side of the lane, dribbled behind his back, faked once and went up. Chalky went up and slapped the ball away. Sam got the loose ball and started his move down the left side of the foul lane. This time he was really going fast and a few people were calling for him to dunk the ball. But instead he got Chalky moving toward the basket, stopped short, and went up for a short jump shot. Only Chalky went up higher, slapped the ball away and then ran around Sam to get it. Chalky dribbled right down the middle of the lane, put a little move on Sam toward the left and then took a big step toward the right and made a lay-up. It was obvious that Chalky was good. Sam took the ball out and threw a jump shot from the top of the key and made it. Chalky did exactly the same thing. Sam took the ball out again and started to make a move down the side of the lane when Chalky took the ball from him and Sam slipped and fell on the seat of his pants. Chalky dribbled back to the foul line and shot a one hander that floated through the air and fell in without touching the rim.

Sam looked over at Clyde when he was taking the ball out, and you could see he was worried. Sam took the ball out, drove down the sideline, and threw up a running hook. The ball bounced off the rim and Chalky grabbed it, bounced the ball once, went up and dunked! When he came down he just handed the ball to Sam. Sam took the ball out and dribbled in close to the basket with his back toward Chalky. He stopped and looked over his left shoulder and then quickly over his right and dribbled to his left, jumped, and shot the ball cleanly through the hoop. Chalky just went and leaned against the wall and shook his head.

"You double dribbled, man," Chalky said.

Sam was about to protest when he looked over at

us and we nodded that he had. Chalky took the ball out and dribbled to the corner, turned and shot a one hander. He missed but he got his own rebound and laid it in.

Sam licked his lips and took a deep breath. He held the ball out of bounds for a few seconds and then started in, but slowly this time. He dribbled in a few steps, stopped, then threw a long jump shot. It went in. Then Chalky took the ball out. But this time Sam was on him. I mean, Sam was ON HIM. Chalky turned right, tried to dribble behind his back, and the ball hit the top of his sneaker and rolled away. Sam had the ball again. Sam took it out and brought the ball to the top of the key, faked to the left, and hit a jumper when Chalky fell back.

Chalky took the ball out and Sam was on him again. Chalky started his dribble and Sam kept hitting the ball. He couldn't get the ball away from Chalky, but Chalky couldn't do much with Sam all over it. Finally Chalky tried to force a jump shot and it hit the backboard and Sam got and made the rebound.

And that's the way the rest of the game went. As long as Sam didn't play a strong defense, Chalky could do his thing. But when Sam got on him, he couldn't do anything. It wasn't easy for Sam to score on Chalky, either, because Chalky was good. But he couldn't play the kind of defense that Sam could. Sam won by four baskets.

Afterwards we all gave Sam five and congratulated

him. Chalky went over to the side and messed with his sneakers.

"Come on," Sam said, "let's go over and sit with Chalky. That guy's a good ballplayer."

"But I think you taught him something tonight, Sam," I said.

"I think we both taught each other something tonight," Sam said. "Big-mouth guys can be into something, too."

So we all went over and sat with Chalky. He was a good ballplayer, but I was still glad Sam won.

Afterwards we had tryouts and the guys I thought I could beat were pretty good. In fact, they were just about as good as me. I was very worried. At the end of the workout Mr. Reese called five of us over and told us that we each had to take four shots from the foul line and that everybody else had already made the team. I made my first shot and then I missed my next two. Everybody had made two shots except me. I was the first one to shoot the fourth shot and I missed. All the others made their shots. Mr. Reese told us to shower and get dressed and report to his office.

I felt terrible. I really felt terrible. Clyde and Sam didn't look at me or anything in the shower room. Then we all got dressed and went into Mr. Reese's office.

"I've decided," he said, "since you're all a pretty good bunch of ballplayers, and since some of you can shoot well and some of you are good ball handlers, to expand the team to seventeen and you guys are going to be my team. First practice Wednesday at six o'clock sharp!"

I had made the team! We all stopped at Freddie's for sodas and I felt so good I forgot that I didn't have any money to pay for the soda. Luckily for me, Chalky had an extra quarter and he lent it to me. I guess he's okay after all.

party time!

11 One day we were all sitting on the stoop and along comes Robin and two other guys from 118th Street. I remembered Robin's fight with Binky when Robin bit a piece of Binky's ear off, and I wondered if there was going to be any trouble. I really didn't think so, though, because three guys didn't usually start anything with three other guys. If I had been there by myself I would have been nervous, though. Robin really looked sharp, too. He had on a pair of green, yellow, and red shoes with high platforms, and a brown suit with a tie, and a handkerchief that matched the shoes.

"Hey, fellas, what's happening?" He looked at us and held out his hand and Clyde gave him five. You could tell Clyde just did it to avoid trouble.

"How's it going, Robin?" Clyde asked.

"Okay, man, okay. Say, look, I'm giving a little thing, you know, a party, and I want you cats to come on around. About ten o'clock this coming Friday evening. And don't bring no chicks because I invited too many chicks already." Then he took out these little squares of paper with the address written on them and gave us all one.

After they had left, Cap threw his slip of paper into the street and so did most of the others, and then we started talking about Robin. Sam said he'd seen Robin driving a car and I said he wasn't old enough to get a license so he couldn't be driving a car.

"You see any glasses on my eyes, man?" Sam asked.

"Maybe you need some," I said. He gave me a look.

"If I say Robin was driving a car the dude was driving a car, that's all. I didn't say he had a driver's license. I didn't say he shops at the A & P. No, all I said was that I saw the dude driving a car. I didn't say nothing about nothing else. Unless you're calling me a liar?"

"If I wanted to call you a liar, Sam," I said, leaning back against the steps as cool as I could, "I'd punch you in the jaw, knock you out, and put a note on your chest for you to read when you woke up."

Sam threw a half punch at me and I moved out the way and made like I was going to hit him in the jaw. I knew that Sam didn't like to fight and that we were only kidding. I also knew that if we weren't kidding I'd be easing my tail off the stoop before Sam knocked *me* out. Anyway, Cap and them left and only me and Sam and Clyde were on the stoop. Me and Sam were more or less talking about how bad we were and what we were going to do if the other guy made the wrong move and that kind of nonsense, when, suddenly, Clyde spoke up.

"I'm going, you know," he said.

"Going where?" Sam asked.

"To Robin's party."

"No lie?"

"Yeah, I'm going."

"How come?" I asked. I was really surprised. No one on the block really liked Robin or the people he hung around with.

"To see what kind of party they give. I don't like Robin but I'd like to know what kind of party they give." Clyde took his paper out of his shirt pocket and looked it over. "If I don't dig the party, then I'll leave."

"I might go, too," Sam said.

"Well, let me know if you're going to go," Clyde said. "I don't really feel like going over there by myself."

"I'll go," Sam answered.

"Me, too," I said.

"You're too young, Stuff," Sam said. "They'll be drinking and everything."

"He can come with us," Clyde said. "We're not going to let anything happen to him."

"Yeah. That's right, I guess."

"You going to tell Kitty you're going?" I asked.

"No," Clyde answered, looking at me. "Why?"

"No reason, I just asked." I knew that if he told Kitty, then Kitty would tell Sharon for sure, and Sharon would tell Mama before her ears cooled off from hearing it. Then I probably wouldn't be able to go. But if I just told my mother I was going to a party with Clyde and Sam she'd let me go. That's what I did and she said okay. She didn't even give me a time to be home.

So we met down at Freddie's and had coffee and then we went over to 118th Street where the party was being held. It was one of those old buildings but it had an elevator. We went up to the ninth floor and as soon as we stepped out of the elevator you could tell where the party was. The whole floor was flooded with sound. We went to the apartment and knocked on the door. I couldn't figure out how the guy who answered the door could have heard us because of all the noise. He opened the door and asked us who we were and we told him and he asked to see our invitations. We said that we didn't have any, only the address. He said that was our invitation, and Clyde and me showed him ours and he let Sam in because Sam was with us. After we got in I saw that he was standing at the door just listening for people who were coming in.

The party was kind of dark. There were a lot of girls there, as Robin had said, and a lot of guys, too.

A guy came over and asked if we wanted some wine, and Clyde said no, maybe a little later, and Sam and me said the same thing. As our eyes became accustomed to the darkness I realized we were the only ones from our block. Some of the other people were actually grownups, although there were a lot of kids, too. Me, Sam, and Clyde stood around for a while and then we danced with some of the girls. Talk about close dancing! The girl I danced with was so close I thought she was trying to get through me. She had been drinking, too, and she started kissing me as we danced. I kissed her back. I didn't even know her but I was kissing her. When the dance was over she said I was real cute and asked me where I lived. I told her and she said that it was a nice block. I asked her where she lived and she said uptown, downtown, and sometimes all around town.

Now what did she mean by that? Uptown, downtown, and sometimes all around town. It had to mean something, right? I didn't know and I decided not to ask. That was the first time I'd danced that close with a girl and the first time I'd kissed a girl I hardly knew. Especially the way we were kissing.

I danced with a lot of girls. So did Clyde and Sam, and the party was all right except a lot of the people were high. Some of the girls were really high and some of the guys, too. Also, I knew that some of the guys were high on smoke. At least I figured they were because I could smell it. Sam said that if I didn't watch out I'd get a contact high. They had a lot of soda and some beer so I drank some soda and had one beer. Clyde had the soda and so did Sam. When they saw me drinking the beer they gave me a look but I ignored them.

The party was getting on pretty late, and I thought perhaps I'd better leave. It was almost one thirty and I knew that usually my mother expected me home, even when I was with Clyde and Sam, by twelve o'clock. I knew I had an excuse because this time she hadn't given me a time to get home. But I also knew that she still expected to see me coming in at a decent time. I also knew that Sharon would be awake. No matter what time I came home she'd be awake to make sure that everyone in the house knew that I had come in late or to ask me what I'd been doing. That's Sharon for you. So I was trying to figure exactly when I was going to leave when Sam came over to me and said that Carnation Charley was there. I hadn't seen him and was surprised. Because Carnation Charley is a dancing freak. I figured I should have seen him during the dancing, especially on the fast numbers. I asked Sam where he was and he said that he was in the next room sitting in the corner and that he was nodding out. He told me and Clyde to go take a look.

We went into the next room and it was actually a bedroom. Most of the coats were on the bed, pushed over to one side, and this guy and girl were on the bed kissing and going on. Over in the corner was Carnation Charley, and you could tell he was high on dope. His eyes were half open and he just sat and rocked a little. Clyde went over to him and asked if he was okay.

"Everything is everything," he said. He kind of scratched at his face and kept on leaning.

"Hey, man, what you guys want? Why don't you do what you want to do and get on out!"

The guy on the bed with the girl said that. I got my coat and Clyde got his. When Sam saw us with our coats he went in and got his. Robin saw us getting ready to leave and came over. He asked us if we wanted to try some dynamite stuff. Clyde said no and Robin said that everything was cool. That if we wanted to later we always could.

"How'd you enjoy the party?" he asked.

"It was okay," Sam said.

"I dug you checking out that chick with the big Fro." Robin smiled. "Hey, dig. I give a little set every Friday night. Why don't you come on around and check it out?"

"Right," Sam said. Except he said it in a long-drawn-out manner like he really wanted to do it. This girl, the one Sam had been dancing with, came over and asked if she could see him again. Sam said yes and then she asked if he lived alone. Sam said no, that he lived with his parents, and she said it was too bad because she would have liked to see him later that night. Then she gave him a little kiss and said that maybe she would see him next week. Then we left.

I got the door open real quiet and the light was on in the kitchen. In my apartment when you open the door you're in the kitchen. Guess who was in the kitchen? Right, my father. Waiting up for me. Only he had fallen asleep sitting at the kitchen table. I sneaked in, quietly tipped through the kitchen and into my room. Just as I got into my room Sharon's radio went on, full blast. It woke my father up and he came running into Sharon's room to see what the matter was.

"I heard somebody in the hallway so I got up and turned the radio on so I could see what time it was and it came on," she said. "I'm sorry."

Then, naturally, my father knew I had just come in.

"What time your mother tell you to be home, boy?"

"She didn't say," I said.

"What do you mean, she didn't say?" He had his shirt off and had a little hole in his T-shirt. I wanted to laugh at that but I knew I'd better not.

"She just didn't say." The door to my parents' bedroom opened and out came my mother. She smiled at me and went into the kitchen. I knew she wasn't happy with me staying out late either—the kitchen clock read two fifteen—but she was happy to see me home. Then Sharon got up and said that she had to go to the bathroom.

"It's two fifteen," she said. "Why, it's almost tomorrow." Then she gave me a look. I would have liked to punch her in the nose just then. Then my father jumps up and starts doing his thing.

"Look at the time! Do you realize what time it is? Do you know that it's after two o'clock in the morning?" He went on and on about that for a while and then jumped down my throat about how I had cigarettes on my breath. Now I've never smoked a cigarette in my entire life, but I had to stand there and listen to him tell me about how I smelled like cigarettes. After about a half hour he finally let me go into my room. I took my clothes off and got into bed but I wasn't particularly sleepy. Sharon went back to her room and soon I heard her bumping into the wall, which meant she was asleep. My mother came in after a while and sat on the edge of the bed.

"Were you smoking?" she asked.

"No," I said, "I've never even smoked one cigarette in my life."

"I didn't think so," she said. "You have a good time at the party?"

"Un-huh."

"Think you're a man now?"

"Well . . ."

She gave me a poke in the side and she kept nudging me with her knuckles until I had to laugh and then she kissed me on the forehead and went out. She was okay. My father's okay, too, in his way. But she's okay in a way you can deal with.

I wasn't sleepy and I started thinking some more about the party. How most of the people were drinking or smoking or something. And I wondered how close that girl would have danced if she'd known me. She really couldn't have danced any closer because she was right against me. At first I'd been embarrassed because I was excited and everything but she still didn't care. When she found that out she just danced even closer. And then there was Charley. I didn't know he fooled around with drugs or anything like that. As a matter of fact I was surprised because I had always thought that if a person fooled around with drugs you could always tell. Of course I hadn't seen Carnation Charley for a long time, since I gave him the money at the dance contest, as a matter of fact, but still, I was surprised. Another thing that bothered me was that afterwards me, Sam and Clyde didn't talk about it. We just all went home. Maybe they had to figure it out, too, the same as me. I hoped we'd talk about it the next day.

Then I must have fallen asleep. Because one minute I was thinking about what had happened and the next morning I woke up and there was Sharon sitting on the edge of the bed with some hot chocolate. Just like that. Poof! No dream, no sleep, nothing. Sometimes I think I don't really sleep. I just lay down, close my eyes, and it's morning. My science teacher said that we dream every night. If she asks it on a test I'll put it down the way she explains it but I don't really believe it.

When I saw Gloria later that day she told me she'd heard that Charley was a junkie. I asked her who she'd heard it from, and she said she'd heard it from Sam. That really annoyed me—that Sam would talk to Gloria about it before he talked to me. I asked Gloria if she wanted to stop at Freddie's for some coffee and I'd tell her what had happened. She said Sam had already told her but she'd go with me to Freddie's for the coffee. Then she asked me why I hadn't gone to basketball practice.

"What practice?" I asked. And then I remembered. Mr. Reese had told us to be in the gym at one o'clock and that we were going to have a two-hour practice session. I told Gloria that I'd see her later. I went upstairs and got my stuff and then ran all the way over to the gym. I had to knock to get in because Mr. Reese was teaching the guys some secret plays and everybody on the team knew them but me. When I came out of the dressing room he looked at his watch and shook his head. I didn't get into too many games anyway. They were practicing like crazy, really. I had never seen such complicated plays. Guys cutting this way and guys cutting that way and one guy starting toward the corner and then backing away just as a decoy. And everybody on the team was making their shots when they got them free. I watched for about fifteen minutes before he finally put me into the game.

"You think you know the three play?" he asked. I said yes and he put me in. I was supposed to get the ball, dribble to the top of the foul circle, and run my man into the center. Then I would either pass the ball to Sam running along the base line or shoot it if I got free. Well, what happened was that I started dribbling, took my eye off the ball for a minute, and Chalky stole it. He threw the ball to Mr. Reese and Mr. Reese just stood and held it.

"This is a serious practice, Stuff!" he said. He threw me the ball again.

This time I kept my body between Chalky and the ball and when I looked up Sam was blocked off. I threw a jump shot from way too far out but it rolled around the rim a couple of times and went in anyway. I really felt good. I asked Mr. Reese was the shot too far out and he said a little.

When the practice was over Mr. Reese told us we could stay in the gym but not to use any of our secret plays in the gym. We just shot around for a while and some other guys came in. One of the other guys was Charley. He shot a few baskets and played some three-man basketball. Clyde and Sam came over to me and said we were going to talk to Charley for a while in the locker room. Jay-Boy, who was Charley's best friend, asked him was anything the matter when

he saw the three of us go into the locker room with
him. Sam told me to take care of Jay-Boy, and I went
over to him and told him to mind his business. I guess
I should have told him something else, like we just
wanted to ask Charley something or something like
that, but I didn't. I thought I could beat Jay-Boy.
Sometimes, when I found I could beat some guy, or
thought I could, I'd just act differently. I'd just act
tougher or something.

When I went into the locker room Charley was
standing up and Sam and Clyde were sitting on the
benches.

"So what you guys want to talk about?" Charley
asked. He was talking tough, like I did when I wasn't
too sure of myself.

"We went to that party the other night," Clyde
said. "And we dug you nodding out."

"Man, what you talking about? You jive dudes
wouldn't know when a cat was nodding out or not."
Charley started on out of the locker room.

"How long you been a junkie, man?" Clyde asked.

Carnation stopped and spun around real quick and
his eyes were popping. I moved away a little but Clyde
stood and moved real close to him.

"Look, Clyde, I don't want to have to kick your
ass," Charley said, "but I will if I have to. You won't
always be with your boys." He looked at me and Sam.

"That's right, Charley. You can do me in. But listen, we got a club, see. . ."

"I don't want to hear about your club, man. I got my own thing."

"And the reason we got this club is to help each other out when we got problems. Why don't you come on and join us, because you got the main qualification, and that's a class-A problem."

Charley stood and walked on toward the door.

"Hey, Charley," Clyde called behind him. "You think you can beat me in a fight?"

"Any day, punk." Charley turned around in the doorway. "Any day."

"I think so, too," Clyde said, "but if you have a problem, I'm still willing to help. So is Sam and so is Stuff or anybody else in the club."

But Charley walked out.

Mr. Reese held practice every day for the next week. Carnation Charley didn't show up even to play three-man basketball after we'd finished our regular practice.

Clyde called a meeting of the Good People and we tried to talk about it. The person who did the most talking was Maria. Maria wasn't too smart. She was smart enough but you wouldn't say she was real smart. But the thing she always did was say things just as they were. If you were asking her about something off the wall she would bring it right down front. And if you were saying one thing and meant something else, she would bring that down front, too. So when we'd been talking about a half hour about what we should do about Carnation Charley, it was Maria who said what we were all thinking about.

"I don't want to be messing with no dope people, not really," she said. "If a guy's a junkie you can't even talk to him unless he's looking at you seeing what he can steal."

"But that's not the point," Clyde said. "If we just walk away from him we're walking away from ourselves. We're all from the same background as Charley, and I don't see how it can't happen to one of us."

"But dope people are rough. And I don't want to get myself killed over anything. Even if I liked the guy, which I really don't care one way or the other, I don't want to get messed up." Maria sat down and looked down at her shoes.

"I know a guy over near Tieman Place that turned in a pusher and got killed," Sam said. "They found his body stuffed in a garbage can and he had about nine bullet holes in his chest."

"What was his name?" Clyde asked.

"I don't know his name but—"

"How did you find out about it?" Clyde continued. "Was it in the paper?"

"I forgot how I found out about it, but they had to cut off his legs to stuff him—"

"Did you see it?"

"No." Sam's voice was lower.

"Then let's stop talking about things we've heard or think we've heard and get down to the problem." Clyde stood up and leaned against the wall. "We either are going to try to help people or we're not. It's as simple as that."

We sat around for a while and thought about what Clyde was saying. It was true that we wanted to help Carnation but we were afraid of people who messed with dope. We had all heard stories about people getting killed or beaten up. Even cops. Maria had said that she was scared of dope people and we all were. Finally Sam said it, too.

"Clyde, I don't want to mess with people in the dope business. And that makes the only thing we can do is to talk to Carnation Charley. I don't think it's really going to do any good. Because anything I say to him he already knows, see. I can say to him that it's bad to be on dope. Don't you think he knows that? I can say, 'Hey, man, dope is gonna make you look bad, feel sad, and get had.' But he knows that, too. I mean, any cat that grows up in this neighborhood knows about what it means to be a junkie. If I've seen one junkie nodding out on some corner I seen a thousand. And old Charley can see as good as me. I know that and you know that and everybody here knows that. So what can we tell him, man? What can we tell him?"

"I don't know," Clyde said.

"Maybe we could tell him to trust in God," Maria said.

"I wish he did, but I really don't know if it would help. But I will tell him if I have the chance, Maria." Clyde looked at her, and I thought she never looked so pretty. "But in case that doesn't work, what shall I tell him?"

"Just tell him that we'll help him if we can, I guess. I know we want to help everybody and everything, but sometimes people get problems you just can't do anything about. I think that's what happens with junkies. They have to get themselves out of it. 'Cause all those drug programs they got don't do that much good. They stay drug-free for a while and then they get right back on it as soon as they leave the program. It's only when they make up their own minds to get off that stuff that they finally do."

We all felt bad about not being able to help Charley. But none of us really knew what to do. You heard about those programs and things but none of us could really do anything about the problem. And as Maria pointed out, most of the programs didn't seem to work too well, either.

It was almost another week when we heard from Carnation Charley again. It was after practice and most of the guys were just sitting around the center drinking Cokes or playing Nok-Hockey when Terry— she's the lady who runs the center's office parts— came in and said that there was an urgent telephone call for Sam. So Sam went into the office and a few minutes later he came out with a slip of paper and called me and Clyde over. He gave the paper to Clyde and we both read the address. It was the same place that we had went to the party before.

"That was some girl named Harriet. She said she was Carnation Charley's girl friend and that he wanted someone to go over to his house and pick up a package that he had left on his dresser and bring it over to this address." Sam looked at Clyde for a reaction. "She said that it was really important for someone to bring the package over or Carnation Charley might get hurt."

We didn't want to go over to his house and get the package, that's for sure. Because if Charley might get hurt, then it stood to reason that we might get hurt, too.

"But, on the other hand, suppose we don't take the package over and he does get hurt?" Clyde asked.

"You want to go to the police?" Sam asked.

"And do what? Say that there's a package on Charley's dresser and that his girl friend said to bring it over to this address? We don't really know what's in the package." Clyde undid his sneakers and took them off. Mr. Reese had been letting us use the lockers with the combination locks and Clyde opened his and put in the sneakers. "And we really don't want to know, I think. If we take the package over and we do get in trouble, we can all be witnesses that we don't know what's in the package."

Sam said that he still didn't want to go. I didn't want to go either but I didn't say anything.

"And how about this place we got to go to?" Sam went on. "It could be a whole dope den or something."

"Could be," Clyde replied.

"That's the place we went to that time when we had the party," I said, "when we first saw Charley nodding."

Clyde looked at the address again and so did Sam.

"Hey, that's right," Clyde said.

"And my mother knows his mother and she knows me and she'll probably give me the package, but I still ain't going," Sam said. "I'm going on out to play some more ball."

"I'm going," Clyde said.

"Man, what do you want to mess around with these dope people for? You don't even like Charley that much."

"You like somebody today and you don't like them tomorrow. You meet somebody and they become your friend and then another year goes by and you don't see them any more or they start doing something different and you meet new friends. But the guy is still people."

"Still a junkie, too."

"Maybe he's not a junkie. Maybe he just tried it that one time."

"Yeah, maybe grits ain't groceries and eggs ain't

poultry, too." Sam pulled up his sweatsocks and headed out the door. "See you guys later."

"I'll go," I said. I don't know why I said that. Maybe it's because I dug Clyde and some of the things he did. Maybe because of what he said about having friends, and all. I don't know. I was sure surprised to hear myself saying I was going to go, though.

"You don't have to go, you know." Clyde looked at me. "My going might be jive, too, but I have to give it a try. If I help Charley, okay, and if I don't, at least I tried. Something I have to do. That make any sense?"

"Yeah."

Clyde smiled.

"Well, if you get it all figured out, will you run it down to me, 'cause I don't really understand it that much."

We changed clothes and went over to Carnation Charley's house. We got the address from the center log book. Everybody in the center had to put their name in the log book. It was only about three blocks and we got there in a couple of minutes. The building was dimly lit and the tin edging on the stairs was coming off. Somebody had written all over the walls, things like Soul Watcher 114 and Taki 182. We got up to Charley's apartment on the third floor. The door was covered with sheet metal, except where the locks and the peep hole were cut out and the apartment number, 5C, was painted in red right below the peephole. Clyde rang the buzzer and a dog started barking. It sounded like a medium-sized dog. A moment later someone asked who it was.

"Clyde Jones, I came over to pick up a package for Charley."

The door opened about an inch while Charley's mother peered at us. I wondered if the peephole was working. Then the door closed and opened again while she took the chain off.

I had seen Charley's mother a lot of times around the neighborhood. I had even borrowed a dime from her once at the laundromat to put into the drier. Only at the time I didn't know it was Charley's mother. She was shorter than Charley and really heavy. And while Charley had a narrow face, she had a wide face that always seemed just about ready to burst into a grin.

"Hi, boys, come on in," she said. "Charley ain't home right now but I guess he'll be home any minute now."

"He's over on 118th Street and he called us and asked if we'd bring a package that was on his dresser over to him," Clyde said.

"He did, did he?" She looked at Clyde and then looked at me, all the while wiping her hands off on a dish towel. "Don't you owe me a dime?"

I nodded my head yes.

"Uh-huh, I thought you were the little rascal. You ain't thinking about leaving town or nothing without paying me my dime, are you?"

"No, ma'am."

"Well, go on into Charley's room and get this mysterious package. How come you young boys and girls got to be so mysterious, anyway?"

"He just told us to get the package," Clyde said.

Clyde and I went into Charley's room and got the package. He had a nice room with pictures of ball-players on the walls and two small trophies. Clyde asked Charley's mother if she wanted to look at the package or anything and she said no, that Charley was so touchy about his privacy.

"I got to knock on the door before I go into the room now. Can you imagine that? That boy's just beginning to smell his own pee and telling me I got to knock on the door?" She was beginning to wash the kitchen floor and had filled a large gray pail with hot, steaming water and ammonia. You could feel the ammonia tingling the inside of your nose. The soapy water made white bubbles on her black hands as she rinsed the mop out. "Just the other day I knocked on the door, didn't really have nothing to say, just wanted to talk to him, and you know what he says when I knock? 'Who's there?' Now just me and him in the house and he's asking who's there. I think that boy don't have a bit of sense sometimes. I really do believe that. You tell him he better get up here in time to do his homework, too."

We left. Soon as we got downstairs we started messing with the package. It was really a paper bag all wrapped up in string. I asked Clyde if he thought it was dope, and Clyde said no, that he thought it

was too heavy to be dope. That was a relief. He told
me to carry it and I took it from him, feeling it as
much as I could, and Clyde was right, it didn't feel
much like dope. Not that I knew what a real bag of
dope felt like, but this was heavier, and a little lump-
ier than I thought dope should be.

We got around to 118th Street and went to the
house where we had been before and where they had
given the party. The same guy that answered the door
when we went to the party that night answered the
door again. I got this picture in my mind of this guy
spending his whole life at the door, waiting for somebody to knock so he could open it and be cool.

"What you guys want?" he asked.

"We got something for Charley," Clyde said, just
about as cool as the guy on the door.

"What you got?"

"What you want to know for?" Clyde asked. Now,
I didn't think that Clyde should have said that. He
could have said "a package" or "something that he
asked us to bring over" or anything but I didn't think
he should be too tough. The guy at the door just
stood and looked at Clyde for a while and Clyde
looked right back at him. Now this guy was maybe
not a complete grownup but he was close enough. He
had a bigger mustache than my father but he looked
young. Finally he moved away from the door and let
us in. That was when we saw Charley.

As soon as I saw Charley, slumped over in this big
stuffed chair, I was scared. Maybe, as Sam says, I get

scared easy, but I had never been so scared as when I saw Charley. He was hunched over in the chair and his breath was coming real hard, as if he had been running for a long time. When he looked up I saw that his nose was running and that some had dried on his face. He was rocking back and forth, and trying to catch his breath, and he looked terrible. I had seen some dead people before, once when a man had been hit by a car and we were waiting around for the ambulance to come and pick him up, and the second time was when I had to go to a funeral because my mother and father were going and they couldn't get a baby-sitter. This was some time ago. Anyway, that's what Charley looked like, a dead man. His face, which was usually shiny and even sweaty, was dull. And the side of his face, just over the cheek, was swollen as if someone had hit him.

"Hi, Charley." Clyde got up his nerve to talk.

Charley looked up at us and motioned toward the door. I looked toward the door and another guy was standing there. He came over and took the package from Clyde. He called the guy that was standing near the door over and he took out a knife and opened the package. It was full of little cellophane packages. The guy looked at them and began to count them. When he finished he smiled and shook his head. Then he pointed at Charley. "Get that punk out of here."

The door guy, who was wearing a jacket, opened it up and there was a gun sticking in his belt. He reached over and grabbed Charley by the collar and jerked him to his feet and pushed him roughly toward the door. Charley took a stumbling step and fell. The guy who had counted the cellophane packages came over to us and put one of the little packages into Clyde's shirt pocket and one into my dungaree pocket and told us to get Charley out of there. I almost peed. I caught it just in time.

We helped Charley up as best we could, Clyde doing most of the lifting, and helped him out of the door. We took him to the elevator. He was able to walk a little and he was crying. By the time we got him down to the first floor, he was able to walk by himself with just Clyde helping him. He was still crying, though, and so was I. We got outside and Clyde told me that he was going to take Charley to his house and for me to go to get Sam. I took off, running. I wasn't only running to get Sam, I was running because I was scared.

I got to Sam's house and tried to tell him what had happened but I couldn't. I tried real hard but I was still crying and I was still scared. Finally Sam got right in front of me, real close, and kept saying where should he go? Where should he go? I told him to go to Clyde's house and he took right off. I started to follow him. I could actually feel my heart beating in my head. He had went down the stairs a half flight at a time and I followed as quickly as I could. By the time I had got to the street he wasn't even in sight.

By the time I got to Clyde's house he had Charley

laying on his bed and he and Sam had taken off Charley's jacket and shirt. Clyde said that BB, Gloria, and Maria were coming over. They got over in no time at all. It looked like the side of Charley's face was swelling even more than it had been before. Sam said we should get Charley up and walk him around so that he didn't die of an overdose. We got him up, which was pretty difficult to do, but then he just threw up, all over me mostly. Sam and Clyde put him back down and Maria helped me clean up while BB and Gloria helped Clyde and Sam. Gloria said that she thought Carnation Charley was going to die. After a while I started to believe her. His breathing was still raspy and his eyes kept rolling around and I knew he couldn't control them. His nose was running, too.

Sam said that we should call the police and have them send up an ambulance, and I thought that was the best thing to do. Clyde wasn't sure and neither was BB and Gloria. Finally Sam asked Clyde if he could use the phone and he called his father. Sam's father was tall and kind of long-headed like Sam and he was about the youngest-looking father on the block. Sam told his father to hurry, that Carnation Charley was OD'ing. Then he had to explain what OD'ing was and he asked him to come right over.

"My daddy is coming over," he said. And he was so calm when he said it that you just knew everything was going to be all right.

Maria got some ice and put it in a towel and placed

it against Charley's cheek where the swelling was. Clyde loosened his clothing and he and Sam kept turning him over every time he had to throw up a little bit of white stuff. When Sam's father got there he took one look at Charley and lifted him to his feet and started shaking him and making him walk. He lifted Charley like Charley was as light as a feather. He told Gloria to put on some coffee and she and BB ran to do it.

"What you boys messin' around with this dope for?" Sam's father's face had a wild look about it and his eyes would catch us and stop us just where we stood. And all the time he talked he kept looking at us the same way and making Charley walk around.

"We weren't fooling around with any dope," Clyde said. "He's the only one that was fooling around with dope. Not us."

"Sam, you ever touch that dope?" Sam's father stopped in the middle of the room and gave Sam a look. He was holding Charley under the arms and the sweat on his forehead ran down and gathered on his eyebrow and would fly off as he jerked his head around, looking from Charley to Sam.

"No, Daddy." Sam's voice went about as high up as it could go. "None of us were fooling around with dope. Really, none of us."

Slowly Charley started coming around again. He began to mumble, and then he seemed scared. Sam's father sat him down in front of the window. When

Charley started coming around and realized where he was, he tried to act cool, but Sam's father took his head between his hands and turned his face up so he could look right into it. Charley struggled for about a few seconds and then he was still when he found out that he couldn't get away. We didn't know what Sam's father was going to do.

"Why you want to die, boy? You tell me that!"

"I don't want to die," Charley said. His voice was weak and he was trying to keep his eyes closed so he wouldn't have to look into Sam's father's face.

"You mess with dope you're going to die. You never see no *old* dope fiend, do you? That's 'cause they all die young. So why you want to die?"

Charley really looked miserable. There was still some mess on the side of his face from where he had been throwing up. He tried to push away the strong hands that were holding him but he couldn't. That was the first time I noticed how badly his hands were swollen. They were puffed up almost twice the size of normal hands.

"Why you want to die, boy?"

The front door opened and Clyde's mother came in with Kitty. When they told her what had happened she just sank into a chair. She didn't seem very upset, just very tired. She did ask if anybody else was involved in the drug thing. Maria said no—I think she was going to say it was just Charley but instead she kind of nodded at him and said, "Only some people."

Mrs. Jones looked up at Clyde and reached out for his hand.

"Hey, Mom, we're all cool." Clyde lifted his mother's face and looked right at her and kissed her.

So we got Charley all right, at least so he could get himself together and go home by himself. Sam's father offered to take him home, but Charley said no, that he'd be all right. When Charley left, Sam's father went to the door with him and watched him as he walked to the staircase. Through the open door I could see Charley go slowly down the hallway and then, as if he felt us watching him, he glanced back for a second and then dropped his head and went off into the night. We all felt a little relieved when Charley left, I guess, but I kept thinking that the club hadn't helped him at all. We had saved his life but I wasn't even sure that was really helping. Sam's father cooled down and we thought everything was okay.

But we hadn't been arrested yet.

I figure that for a guy of thirteen I'd spent a lot of time in jail. There was that time when Binky and Robin had a fight and we took Binky's piece of ear to the hospital and got taken down to jail. That was about an hour. Then there was the time that Sam and Clyde and me got taken down to jail when we got that lady's purse back from the purse-snatchers. That was almost three hours. And then there was the night we helped Charley.

I got home and I was in my room telling Sharon

what had happened. My father had to work late and I was going to tell my mother, but Sharon wanted to know about it first so she could tell her friends. Anyway, I told her not to tell anybody because it wasn't anybody's business except the people who were actually there. Also, I didn't want to be the first to tell everybody if Clyde and Sam didn't tell. But I was telling Sharon when all of a sudden I heard voices in the hallway. Then there was a key in the door and my father came in with two policemen.

"Boy!" my father called out to me. I saw the policemen with him, and I thought he was in trouble. So I went on out into the kitchen where they were. "You been messing around with any dope?"

"No." I said.

"Let's see your arms." One of the policemen grabbed my wrist and started pushing up my sleeve.

"Take your hands off my boy!" My father's voice came out so loud it scared me. "He can roll his own sleeve up. Roll your sleeve up, son."

I rolled up my sleeves and started to cry at the same time. I don't know why I always start to cry at the least little thing, but I sure did. I rolled up my sleeves and the policeman looked at my arms and then he looked at my eyes. Then he took out a picture and showed it to my father and asked if that was me in the picture. My father said yes, it was me, and the policeman said I'd have to come downtown with him. My mother, who was standing in the doorway all the time, looked at me and her eyes were as wide as anything. Her lip was quivering, too, and I just started into crying more. I hadn't done anything but I just kept crying. My father got on his coat and he said he was going with me.

"You can meet us down at the precinct," the policeman said. "You know where the Twenty-eighth is?"

"I'm going down with the boy." My father said it again and I know he meant it. The policemen looked at each other and shrugged.

My mother asked to see the picture, and I saw it, and it was a picture of me and Clyde helping Carnation Charley down from the house on 118th Street. I didn't remember seeing anyone taking our pictures, really, and I don't know where it could have come from.

My father and I sat in the back of the police car while the two policemen sat in the front. Oh, yes, when we came downstairs all the neighbors were standing around watching. They were saying things like 'Hey, ain't that Mrs. Williams' boy?' They knew who I was. They just wanted something to talk about, that's all.

All the way down to the police station my father had his arm around me. He said that no matter what happened he was on my side. I told him that I didn't do anything and he said, "Good." I don't ever remember him putting his arm around me like that before. I wish we hadn't been in the police car when he did it.

When we got to the police station we had to go

up to the second floor. Everybody was there. They had Clyde, Sam, Charley, Robin, the guy that was in the apartment with Robin, and about five other guys I didn't even know. Everybody had on handcuffs except Clyde. Even Sam had on handcuffs. One policeman, who was dressed in ordinary clothes instead of a uniform, told the policemen who brought us in to take me into another room. My father said he was coming with me. We went into a small dark room and the policeman told me that I didn't have to say anything if I didn't want to and if I wanted a lawyer they would get one for me. I told him I didn't do anything and he said he didn't think I had. Then he told me to tell him the whole story about us going into that building today.

So I did. I told him about us getting the phone call from Carnation's girl friend and us going over to this house. I even told him about the party that I had went to before, and the policeman asked me if I had ever smoked a reefer. I said no, that I didn't smoke. Then he went over to the wall and pulled back a curtain and told me that it was a one-way mirror. He told me to look through it and see if I knew anybody that was in the other room. I told him I knew Sam and Clyde and Carnation and Robin but that I really didn't know anybody else they had there.

Then they brought in Gloria's father and mother and I said I knew them, too. They put us all into a big room with about four policemen and we weren't allowed to talk to each other or sit next to each other. Sam still had the handcuffs on. Finally they came and took away Robin and his friends, or at least I guess they were his friends because I didn't know any of them. They took Carnation Charley, too. They told the rest of us we could go. When we went downstairs all the rest of the parents—Clyde's mother, Sam's parents, and everybody—were downstairs.

Then a policeman came and told us that they had just broken up a drug ring that was getting a lot of kids messed up in the neighborhood. That the police had been photographing everyone that went into the building and that they had just picked up everybody to check them out. They were just about ready to let us go when one of the detectives asked Clyde if we had any dope. Clyde said, to my surprise, that we did. He said that the guy at Robin's place had given him some and me some. Then he took his out of his shirt pocket and gave it to him and then the detective came over to me and I looked in my shirt pocket and mine was gone. I could have died. I looked in my pants pockets and then my shirt pocket again but it still wasn't there.

"Did your mother give you your shirt to put on?" a detective asked me. I told him yes while I kept looking through my pockets. He left the room and came back a few minutes later. He had checked with my mother and she had said that she had given me a clean shirt to put on and he sent her home to look in my other shirt pocket. It took her almost an hour to get back, but she brought the other shirt. The detective looked into the pocket and there it was. What a relief. Then they told us that we probably wouldn't have to testify at a trial or anything but that we might and not to leave town or anything. Then they let us go.

When I got home, first, of course, I had to get my lecture from my father about the next time something happened I was supposed to tell him about it first. And then I got lecture number two about how bad dope was and how I should stay away from people who offered me dope and how some people were just looking for kids to mess with and everything. He didn't really have to tell me that. I mean, I saw Charley and I saw everything that was going on and, after all, I had been in jail.

I didn't get any sleep for the rest of the night, hardly. Sharon came sneaking into my room and I had to tell her all about going to jail. She asked if BB or Maria or Gloria had to go to jail, and I told her no and she seemed relieved. I think she didn't want to be the only girl left out.

We were coming home from practice two days later when we saw Carnation Charley again. He came over to us and said hello and everything and we said hello. He said that he was in a rehabilitation program and that he had finished with drugs for good. They were giving him something to help him get off whatever it was he was taking and also helping him to get his credits for high school. Sam said that he should really stay away from drugs because it really messed him around.

"We thought you was going to die, man," Sam said, "you were about that close to being gone."

"I'm hip." Carnation Charley leaned against a lamppost and talked to us. "You know, I realized that if I'm ever going to make anything of myself—well, that's not the way. What I'm going to do now is to finish school and try to get into this program they have over at the State Employment place—it's a earn-while-you-learn thing—and work there long enough to get money for college. Then when I get into college I'll probably go out of state and get a degree in accounting or something like that. That's what they were saying over to the place where I'm in this program. They were saying that if you get into accounting you're okay because any business you get into has an accountant."

He went on talking about what his plans were and what he was going to do. After a while he said that he was looking into the possibility of getting a scholarship for music at a school in New Mexico. He said that sometimes they give scholarships for singing.

You know, when we were trying to get him to breathing and everything up at Clyde's house that time I didn't really feel sorry for him. I would have, maybe, if I'd thought about it. But I guess I was too

busy or too upset to think about feeling sorry at the
time. But when he was standing on the corner talking
to us, I really felt sorry for him for the first time. He
was saying things that he wanted to do and I knew
he wasn't going to do most of those things at all.
Carnation Charley wasn't even in an academic program and the chances were that he wasn't going to
college at all. But he kept making up things, telling
us that he was, and it was almost like he was begging
us to believe him. I wanted to believe him, I really
did. But I didn't and I didn't know what he was going
to do with his life or where he was going. It was a
funny feeling, because I didn't feel sorry for what he
was doing right then but for his future.

the game

12 *We had practiced and practiced until it ran out of our ears.* Every guy on the team knew every play. We were ready. It meant the championship. Everybody was there. I never saw so many people at the center at one time. We had never seen the other team play but Sam said that he knew some of the players and that they were good. Mr. Reese told us to go out and play as hard as we could every moment we were on the floor. We all shook hands in the locker room and then went out. Mostly we tried to ignore them warming up at the other end of the court but we couldn't help but look a few times. They were doing exactly what we were doing, just shooting a few lay-ups and waiting for the game to begin.

They got the first tap and started passing the ball

around. I mean they really started passing the ball around faster than anything I had ever seen. Zip! Zip! Zip! Two points! I didn't even know how they could *see* the ball, let alone get it inside to their big man. We brought the ball down and one of their players stole the ball from Sam. We got back on defense but they weren't in a hurry. The same old thing. Zip! Zip! Zip! Two points! They could pass the ball better than anybody I ever saw. Then we brought the ball down again and Chalky missed a jump shot. He missed the backboard, the rim, everything. One of their players caught the ball and then brought it down and a few seconds later the score was 6-0. We couldn't even get close enough to foul them. Chalky brought the ball down again, passed to Sam cutting across the lane, and Sam walked. They brought the ball down and it was 8-0.

They were really enjoying the game. You could see. Every time they scored they'd slap hands and carry on. Also, they had some cheerleaders. They had about five girls with little pink skirts on and white sweaters cheering for them.

Clyde brought the ball down this time, passed into our center, a guy named Leon, and Leon turned and missed a hook. They got the rebound and came down, and Chalky missed a steal and fouled his man. That's when Mr. Reese called time out.

"Okay, now, just trade basket for basket. They make a basket, you take your time and you make a basket—don't rush it." Mr. Reese looked at his starting five. "Okay, now, every once in a while take a look over at me and I'll let you know when I want you to make your move. If I put my hands palm down, just keep on playing cool. If I stand up and put my hands up like this"— he put both hands up near his face—"that means to make your move. You understand that?"

Everyone said that they understood. When the ball was back in play Chalky and Sam and Leon started setting picks from the outside and then passed to Clyde for our first two points. They got the ball and started passing around again. Zip! Zip! Zip! But this time we were just waiting for that pass underneath and they knew it. Finally they tried a shot from outside and Chalky slapped it away to Sam on the break. We came down real quick and scored. On the way back Mr. Reese showed everybody that his palms were down. To keep playing cool.

They missed their next shot and fouled Chalky. They called time out and, much to my surprise, Mr. Reese put me in. My heart was beating so fast I thought I was going to have a heart attack. Chalky missed the foul shot but Leon slapped the ball out to Clyde, who passed it to me. I dribbled about two steps and threw it back to Leon in the bucket. Then I didn't know what to do so I did what Mr. Reese always told us. If you don't know what to do then, just move around. I started moving toward the corner and then I ran quickly toward the basket. I saw Sam coming at me from the other direction and it was a play. Two guards cutting past and one of the defensive men gets picked off. I ran as close as I could to Sam, and his man got picked off. Chalky threw the ball into him for an easy lay-up. They came down and missed again but one of their men got the rebound in. We brought the ball down and Sam went along the base line for a jump shot, but their center knocked the ball away. I caught it just before it went out at the corner and shot the ball. I remembered what Mr. Reese had said about following your shot in, and I started in after the ball but it went right in. It didn't touch the rim or anything. Swish!

One of their players said to watch out for 17—that was me. I played about two minutes more, then Mr. Reese took me out. But I had scored another basket on a lay-up. We were coming back. Chalky and Sam were knocking away just about anything their guards were throwing up, and Leon, Chalky, and Sam controlled the defensive backboard. Mr. Reese brought in Cap, and Cap got fouled two times in two plays. At the end of the half, when I thought we were doing pretty well, I found out the score was 36–29. They were beating us by seven points. Mr. Reese didn't seem worried, though.

"Okay, everybody, stay cool. No sweat. Just keep it nice and easy."

We came out in the second half and played it pretty cool. Once we came within one point, but then

they ran it up to five again. We kept looking over
to Mr. Reese to see what he wanted us to do and
he would just put his palms down and nod his head
for us to play cool. There were six minutes to go when
Mr. Reese put me and another guy named Turk in.
Now I didn't really understand why he did this because I know I'm not the best basketball player in
the world, although I'm not bad, and I know Turk
is worse than me. Also, he took out both Sam and
Chalky, our two best players. We were still losing by
five points, too. And they weren't doing anything
wrong. There was a jump ball between Leon and their
center when all of a sudden this big cheer goes up
and everybody looks over to the sidelines. Well, there
was Gloria, BB, Maria, Sharon, Kitty, and about four
other girls, all dressed in white blouses and black skirts
and with big T's on their blouses and they were our
cheerleaders. One of their players said something stupid about them but I liked them. They looked real
good to me. We controlled the jump and Turk drove
right down the lane and made a lay-up. Turk actually
made the lay-up. Turk once missed seven lay-ups in
a row in practice and no one was even guarding him.
But this one he made. Then one of their men double-
dribbled and we got the ball and I passed it to Leon,
who threw up a shot and got fouled. The shot went
in and when he made the foul shot it added up to
a three-point play. They started down court and Mr.
Reese started yelling for us to give a foul.

"Foul him! Foul him!" he yelled from the sidelines.

Now this was something we had worked on in practice and that Mr. Reese had told us would only work once in a game. Anybody who plays basketball knows that if you're fouled while shooting the ball you get two foul shots and if you're fouled while not shooting the ball you only get one. So when a guy knows you're going to foul him he'll try to get off a quick shot. At least that's what we hoped. When their guard came across the mid-court line, I ran at him as if I was going to foul him. Then, just as I was going to touch him, I stopped short and moved around him without touching him. Sure enough, he threw the ball wildly toward the basket. It went over the base line and it was our ball. Mr. Reese took me out and Turk and put Sam and Chalky back in. And the game was just about over.

We hadn't realized it but in the two minutes that me and Turk played the score had been tied. When Sam and Chalky came back in they outscored the other team by four points in the last four minutes. We were the champs. We got the first-place trophies and we were so happy we were all jumping around and slapping each other on the back. Gloria and the other girls were just as happy as we were, and when we found that we had an extra trophy we gave it to them. Then Mr. Reese took us all in the locker room and shook each guy's hand and then went out and invited the parents and the girls in. He made a little speech about how he was proud of us and all, and not just because we won tonight but because we had worked so hard to win. When he finished everybody started clapping for us and, as usual, I started boo-hooing. But it wasn't so bad this time because Leon started boo-hooing worse than me.

You know what high is? We felt so good the next couple of days that it was ridiculous. We'd see someone in the street and we'd just walk up and be happy. Really. And even the people on the team or who weren't in the Good People or anything. Everybody was just so happy. And things started happening that made us even more happy. Well, what actually happened was that we got our report cards again and Clyde got some really good marks. They weren't in the nineties but every single one of them was in the eighties. His grade adviser called him down to the office and told him how hard it was going to be for him in summer school and all but that he thought Clyde could do it if he really tried.

Clyde said that he got mad because he was saying that he couldn't graduate just a little while ago and he still didn't say anything about what made the difference. But that wasn't even the best news. It didn't help that we all thought that Clyde was going to make it—we just took it for granted that he was, but it didn't help him. But no one thought that Sam was going to college. Especially Sam.

Sam came running down the block and screaming and carrying on and talking about how great he was.

His voice went way up and he could hardly talk he was so excited. Finally Clyde made him sit down and Gloria sat on his lap while BB read the letter he was carrying.

It was from the University of Arizona and it was offering Sam a full athletic scholarship to play baseball. And Sam didn't even think that baseball was one of his good sports. It was such a good thing that we decided to have a party right then and there. We got all our money together and bought some cookies and chips and things and took them all up to Angel's house because Angel's mother always had something to eat. And we all had the cakes and sodas and some saffron rice and sausages that Angel's mother made and we just felt good. Gloria called it a living high. We went from being happy to feeling great and then to feeling almost silly we were so happy. It was just so good. It was one of the happiest times that I had ever had. We started calling up everybody we knew and told them to come on over to Angel's house. When Angel's father came home and saw the party he called in some of his Puerto Rican friends and they played guitars and sang.

We were all slapping each other on the back and laughing when Maria, who had gone into the bedroom with Gloria, came back crying. She said that Gloria was in her bedroom crying and that it had made her sad. We went in and asked her what the matter was.

"Nothing," she said. She was smiling but her face was streaked with where she had wiped away the tears.

"Do you feel okay?" I asked.

"Yeah!" She stood up and had a big smile on her face and turned to us so that we could see that she wasn't unhappy. But her shoulders began to heave gently and her eyes filled with tears. She fell back onto the bed and cried into the blanket. "I just wish my father would come back!"

She kept saying it over and over again, only you couldn't make out all the words as she cried them into the bed. Suddenly things didn't seem as happy any more. Even the things that looked as if they'd worked out were suddenly less real, less sure. Clyde's passing, which seemed like a sure entry into college a few minutes before, now seemed just a chance. A maybe thing.

It was almost eight thirty when Sharon and I got home and I told my mother what had happened. I told her about Sam getting the scholarship and about Clyde having a chance to get an academic diploma and about Gloria. I got a mini-lecture from my father about how things work out if you study and pay attention in school.

"What about Gloria?" I asked. "What about her?"

I was immediately sorry for saying that. I knew his lectures were meant to help me and all but I just wasn't in the mood to hear his same-old-thing speeches. I tried to cover it up a little by asking him who had won the ball game. I guess I didn't cover it up very well because he answered me.

"It doesn't always work out, I guess. But what are you going to do, believe that it's not going to work out from the start? So maybe it'll work out and maybe it won't. Things don't work out for everybody." He took his handkerchief out of his pocket and blew his nose. "Maybe things that don't work out for some might work for others. Gloria's getting some tough breaks. I had a few tough breaks and things didn't work out so good for me, either. Well, maybe you'll get the breaks. Who knows?"

He stood up and went into the living room and a moment later I heard the television come on. I looked at my mother. She had a faraway look in her eye for a moment and then she looked at me and smiled.

"Getting to be a man, aren't you, boy?"

carnation charley

13 *At first it started as a rumor the next day in school. But when we got out in the afternoon* we found out that it was true. Carnation Charley was dead. They said that he'd been downtown and had tried to rob a store. The owner of the store had set off an alarm and the police came just as he was leaving. They had chased him two blocks and then had shot him to death.

He had said he was through with drugs but when we read about him in the paper the next day they said he was an addict. They said the storekeeper had recognized him as an addict and had triggered the alarm the moment Carnation Charley had entered the store.

I thought about Charley running from the police.

I wondered if he was afraid. I tried to feel what he felt as he ran and I was sad for him. It had happened so far away from where he lived, among strangers, and strange places. And I thought that dying must be strange. That it must be something that he couldn't have understood much more than I understood it. I cut the newspaper article out and saved it and read it over and over again. I found out that Clyde had cut it out, too.

We all went to his funeral and said good-bye to him. He was the first one of us who had died, and even though he wasn't among our close friends it seemed as if it meant that we could all die and that was a sad thing. Because we were all beginning to like each other and like living so much. It was a sad thing that we could die. I felt sorry for me and for Clyde and Sam and BB and Gloria and all of us, just the way I felt sorry for Carnation Charley.

Clyde called another meeting of the Good People after the funeral and he said that, no matter what happened to Charley, we were for real. That even if we couldn't do anything for Charley to save him from being a junkie, or from dying, that at least he must have known that we did care for him.

I wonder what Carnation Charley thought of when he was dying. If he thought of his mother, maybe, or any of us? I don't think so. I think he was just very lonely and afraid. Because that's probably how you die.

We started a softball team that summer and entered a tournament. We had about twelve guys on the team and two girls, BB and Maria. The league told us that if we had girls playing we'd forfeit all of them because of our two girls. We really didn't care. Because they meant more to us than the rules did or than winning did. Oh, yes, I also got a letter from Mr. Brechstein saying that I did not qualify for the school band. As good as I played he must have been out of his mind.

epilogue

The year that Carnation Charley died I think I
jumped a year. The calendar didn't say that I was any
older but I seemed older to me. I think all of us did.
You could kind of see it during that summer. Clyde
finished up high school with really good grades and
Sam took some summer courses that he didn't have
to, just to help himself in areas where he felt kind
of weak. Sharon was sick a lot over the summer and
so I stayed home more than I would have normally.
I kept playing the saxophone and my father bought
me a flute. I didn't even ask him but he said that
a good sax player usually doubled on flute. Then he
gave me this long lecture about how he had never had
anything really good when he was a kid and all and
how I should be grateful. It was a two-hour lecture.
Can you believe that? Two hours!

It was really a funny thing, too, because I hadn't even asked him for the flute. He started talking and talking and I began to feel that he couldn't stop. He just had to go on. And then I realized that I was right. He did have to go on. And he kept saying a lot of jive things about how hard he had it as a kid and how I should really practice a lot because that's the only way I could really be good and things like that. But what had really happened was that he had thought about me and done something really nice for me. That was the flute-buying part. And I got the feeling that he wanted to say something like how he felt about me but just couldn't get it out. So he just kept talking about what I should do as he tried to work his way up to saying something like he liked me. I guess it's hard for people, some people anyway, to say things like that. Maybe we all need Good People clubs.

You know what I did? I helped him. It was funny because he's my father, yet I was helping him.

"I really think you care a lot for me, Pop," I said, but I couldn't look at him. "And I'm glad because I really care for you, too."

"What're you talking about?" he asked in this rough voice. "Just take care of the flute."

He went on into the living room and turned on the television without saying anything else. Later my mother came into my room and said thanks. I asked her for what and she said for whatever it was I said to my father. She can be cool when she wants to, too.

Another thing that happened that same summer was that they tore down some buildings in the next block and made new projects. This didn't seem like much but it was really an important thing. The neighborhood started to change. When all the new people moved in we ended up going to school about a half mile away. We had to take a bus to get there. And slowly the things that made the neighborhood changed and it wasn't the same. I think it had something to do with the new buildings and the fact that new people replaced Clyde and Sam and them in my life. Oh, I still see Clyde when he comes in from school. He dropped out a year and then went back because of money troubles. Sam I see in the summer and sometimes at track meets. He plays baseball in school and runs track. He thinks he's going to play with the major leagues someday. I haven't seen Gloria but, as I told you, I found out that she got married.

The one thing I won't forget is how close we all were. How much we cared for each other. I just hope I'll always have people to care for like that and be close to. And I'd like to be able to teach somebody else that feeling.

Do you know what I wonder? I wonder if sometimes any of the Good People sit around, wherever they are, and say, "Hey, remember old Stuff?" I bet they do.